———◄●►———

For my editor,
Caitlyn,
my most stalwart
Guardian and friend

———◄●►———

Contents

THE GUARDIANS

JACK FROST

THE END BECOMES

THE BEGINNING

THE GUARDIANS

JACK FROST

THE END BECOMES

THE BEGINNING

◆—◆—◆

WILLIAM JOYCE

𝒜
atheneum

A Caitlyn Dlouhy Book

ATHENEUM BOOKS FOR YOUNG READERS

NEW YORK • LONDON • TORONTO • SYDNEY • NEW DELHI

𝒜
atheneum

Atheneum Books for Young Readers
An imprint of Simon & Schuster Children's Publishing Division
1230 Avenue of the Americas, New York, New York 10020

This book is a work of fiction. Any references to historical events, real people, or real places are used fictitiously. Other names, characters, places, and events are products of the author's imagination, and any resemblance to actual events or places or persons, living or dead, is entirely coincidental.

For information about special discounts for bulk purchases, please contact Simon & Schuster Special Sales at 1-866-506-1949 or business@simonandschuster.com.
The Simon & Schuster Speakers Bureau can bring authors to your live event. For more information or to book an event, contact the Simon & Schuster Speakers Bureau at 1-866-248-3049 or visit our website at www.simonspeakers.com.
Also available in an Atheneum Books for Young Readers hardcover edition
Book design by Lauren Rille
The text for this book was set in Adobe Jensen Pro.
The illustrations for this book were rendered in a combination of charcoal, graphite, and digital media.
Manufactured in the United States of America
0720 MTN
First Atheneum Books for Young Readers paperback edition September 2020
10 9 8 7 6 5 4 3 2 1
CIP data for this book is available from the Library of Congress:
ISBN 978-1-4424-3056-3 (hc)
ISBN 978-1-4424-3057-0 (pbk)
ISBN 978-1-4814-1554-5 (eBook)

The Guardians in 1933

The Man in The Moon

Nicholas St. North

Queen Toothiana

E. Aster Bunnymund

Sandman

Our Heroes and Villain in 1933

Katherine
(Mother Goose)

Jackson Overland Frost

Twiner

Pitch

Emily Jane
(Mother Nature)

Jack Frost

CHAPTER ONE

A Nose Is Nearly Nipped

CHRISTMAS EVE WAS JACK'S favorite day of the year. And for the last few decades or so, he had spent that day in his favorite place: his tree.

Jack's tree was the oldest in Central Park. A thousand people, maybe more, walked past it daily and had done so for many years, but not one of them knew that Jackson Overland Frost was very often living inside it.

This tree was much older than the park it stood in and was even older than the city of New York itself. It was a sapling when the city was still called New Amsterdam and there were more Native Americans than settlers living in the swampy forests of Manhattan Island.

By this Christmas Eve 1933, millions of people lived within shouting distance of this noble oak, but its secrets were still more absolute than they had been when flintlocks or bows and arrows were the order of the day.

A heavy snow was falling over all of the East. It muffled the sounds of the city, though New York was already quieting down. People had finished shopping and were heading to their apartments and penthouses and homes. Jack, however, could feel the thrum of excitement from the children. Sleep would be difficult for them. It was, after all, Christmas Eve.

A busy night for Sandman, he thought.

The inside of Jack's tree contained more than a dozen rooms within its majestic hollow, and the furnishings were a mix of pieces from several centuries: spears, shields, stools, and pottery from the various tribes of the Iroquois, along with colonial tables and ornate chairs and couches brought over from Europe. There was a tomahawk from a chief of the Algonquians. The jacket that George Washington had worn the night he crossed the Delaware was hanging on a hat rack that had belonged to Teddy Roosevelt. This tree, like all the tree-houses Jack called home, was a handsome, comfortable clutter of the region's history.

Jack was readying to meet up with the other Guardians when he felt the dull, worrying ache in his left hand. He wanted to ignore it. He knew Nicholas

St. North would already be grumping about his being late.

Jack Frost! The fair-weather Guardian! North would playfully gripe. *Comes and goes when he pleasies!*

The word, my dear North, is "pleases," E. Aster Bunnymund would correct.

Go lay an egg, General Rabbit Bunny, North would retort, and they would begin to amiably argue.

Jack could imagine it exactly. He grabbed his staff, Twiner, and prepared to leave, but then paused as another even sharper pain seared through his hand. He looked at his palm, at the curious scar etched across it. The inky stain of Pitch's blood had discolored it and was, Jack knew, the source of the pain, for it only twinged when Pitch or his forces posed a threat.

He turned back to a cabinet, well hidden, where he

kept his daggers. There were several similar daggers in this secret cabinet. All of them were made from large, sharp, single diamonds, and each gemstone had been formed from the tears of someone Jack had loved. As far back as his earliest days as Nightlight, Jack had possessed the ability to turn sorrow into a weapon. These daggers could only be used against dark forces or to protect the kind and weak. But there was one dagger, unfinished, that was different from the others. It had come from the tears of Pitch himself. This dagger had one purpose only.

Jack had never completed its construction, but he knew now in his heart that it was finally time to use it. And this worried him deeply as he took the dagger and tucked it into its sheath. He slipped on his blue hoodie, which he wore as a sort of uniform, then set out for the pole. The North Pole.

The thousand or so squirrels that sheltered in his tree were eating nuts and singing squirrel carols around a squirrel version of a Christmas tree, a cone-shaped mound of acorns covered with candles. They squealed "Merry Christmas" to him in squirrel-speak. Jack squealed back; he spoke fluent squirrel and chipmunk.

As he leaped out of the hollow, he felt his hand throb once more. *Not now. Not tonight.* He gave his hand a shake.

A breeze suddenly kicked up. The trees swayed and lurched, their message clear. Danger was near. Twiner instantly transformed into a bow and a quiver full of gnarled arrows.

Jack quickly nocked an arrow.

"Where?" he whispered to the bow.

He let Twiner lead him to where he needed to aim.

While Jack could sense danger, Twiner could always see where it was coming from. The wind stilled, and the snow stopped.

Hmmm. Not only do the trees know there's danger, so does Mother Nature. Jack squinted through the trees and spotted something flying through the air toward him.

Nightmare Men! And they were coming fast.

But before Jack could shoot, he heard a telltale sound that made him tense up: the quick, sharp rip of arrows in the air. The limbs closest to him shook and bent faster than seemed possible, forming a shield. Bark and wood took the heavy hits, stopping more than two dozen dark arrows in midflight. One struck less than an inch from Jack's head.

The arrows were most unusual: black as coal, with an oily shine. He had first seen arrows like these back when he had been called Nightlight. These were the very type used in the last great battle against Pitch: the Battle of Bright Night. They came from the Dark Side of the Moon. He pulled his bow tight, whispered "Seek," and let his own arrow fly. It splintered into a multitude of shafts. In the distance he heard a rat-a-tat of thuds as each arrow found its mark. Silence followed. Then the snow began to fall again, Mother Nature's signal that the danger had been dealt with.

In the distance he could just barely hear carolers. They were singing "God Rest Ye Merry, Gentlemen." It was one of his favorites. He looked more closely at the arrow that had nearly killed him.

"Jack Frost nearly had his nose nipped," he said to Twiner. Then he leaped into the air and flew off into the night sky toward the North Pole with a new urgency.

He knew that these arrows meant that Pitch was somehow enacting a long-festering plan of vengeance.

This Christmas would mean the return of the Nightmare King.

CHAPTER TWO

Less Than Early Frost

KATHERINE STOOD WITH KAILASH, her giant Himalayan Snow Goose. They were perched at the top of the actual North Pole. Katherine was anxiously scanning the busy skies for any sign of Jack. Down below, the Great City of Santa was at the height of busyness.

North was bellowing orders from his balcony with the voice amplifier Bunnymund had invented for him. Every citizen of the city who had ears could hear the great man's voice.

"A dream come true for dear North," Bunnymund had said to the others when he had first presented the

amplifier to his fellow Guardian. "An earache for the rest of us."

But if North was urgent in his orders, he was also jolly.

"Get that shipment of teddy bears sorted properly, or I'll stuff you all!" he ordered with a belly laugh. A frantic troop of elves had arrived with a fresh shipment from the Bear Works building. North chuckled at their hurrying.

His laugh was of such full and rumbling mirth that it was rumored to cause earthworms as far away as South America to wiggle underground from the tickling sensation it caused. And so, as the last-minute preparations for the Great Delivery were being put into place, the citizens of the North Pole were in a festive, cheerful panic.

Soon the ten thousand balloon

blimps would be launched to their assigned locations across the globe with their resupplies of toys for North's sleigh. An equal number of Bunnymund's underground trains, also loaded with playthings, would simultaneously steam toward their destinations in many lands.

Of course, sending toys to children across the planet in a single night was a major undertaking, and a certain amount of chaos was to be expected. Yetis were yelling at elves. Elves were shouting at Lunar Lamas. Stuffed animals were nearly at war with toy soldiers. But somehow, with North's urging and good humor, it always seemed to miraculously come together. Every year Katherine was amazed that the scheme worked. *Doing a great kindness to children brings out the best in every creature,* she thought. *But where is Jack tonight?* She always knew when he was in trouble. And tonight the trouble she sensed was deep.

CHAPTER THREE

Pitch Is No Longer at Bat . . . for Now

PITCH DESPISED HIS IMPRISONMENT. It had been more than a hundred years since the Nightmare King had been jailed after the Battle of Bright Night, but his influence had not stopped. His armies had been soundly defeated, but they had not been obliterated. While Pitch did not know how many of his soldiers had escaped, this much was certain: The Earth has many places where shadows and gloom can give safe refuge to wickedness.

His daughter, Emily Jane, had betrayed him, and during these many years since Bright Night, she had

fully evolved into her great calling: to be Mother Nature. While she had stayed neutral throughout the early Nightmare Wars, she now used her formidable powers to keep her father confined.

No jailer in history understood their prisoner's strengths, weaknesses, or abilities better than Emily Jane Pitchiner. She was the only child of Lord Pitchiner, the Golden Age hero who had become the scourge of a thousand galaxies, known as Pitch Black the Nightmare King, and she knew what a valiant and doting father he once was. She knew the tenderness that had once emanated from him. And she knew that in one hand he still held the remains of her childhood portrait in a miniature cameo. Emily Jane clung to the small, desperate hope that he could someday be restored to his former gallant self.

For generations, her father's Nightmare soldiers

had huddled in ragtag groups without their leader, but in time they set about on Nightmare missions that were becoming increasingly more organized and effective. The world seemed to be unraveling, and there was fear in the air. The Nightmare soldiers fed off fear; this made them more daring and powerful. Fear is always a tonic to the wicked. It is dark and stealthy and can travel like no other feeling. Even in his isolation, Pitch could feel this fear.

Pitch's prison was unlike any that had ever been, and it was in the most unlikely of places: underneath the village of Santoff Claussen. So much of the Guardians' history originated from this enchanted settlement, and though it had been a place of refuge for magical thinking and innovation, it was by accidental design the perfect place to contain evil.

It had been Ombric Shalazar, when he was a

young wizard, who had discovered a strange, parched meteor crater at the edge of the European wildlands. The crater's surface was coated with the densest metallic ore he had ever seen, and being the last living citizen of Atlantis, he had seen many things no other being since had laid eyes upon.

In the center of this crater grew a tiny sapling. Tempered by the fires of the cosmos, this tree would soon grow into the towering heart of the village Ombric founded, Santoff Claussen. Its branches, trunk, and roots could transform in density and shape at Ombric's command. Chairs, doors, entire rooms would take shape inside its massive trunk. Ombric called the tree Big Root, and from within this living tree-house, Ombric studied until he was the last of the all-powerful wizards. In time he brought to his town of Santoff Claussen other like-minded men, women, and creatures, and finally, the Guardians themselves. First North and Katherine, who became his pupils. Then Bunnymund, who had knowledge beyond even Ombric's. And Queen Toothiana, and lastly, Sanderson Mansnoozie.

The creature called Nightlight had been in their company from the very beginning. He was the only one who understood Pitch's one weakness—that his villainous heart still had a glimmer of humanity—but this knowledge put Nightlight in constant peril. Pitch hated this weakness, but even more, he hated that Nightlight used it again and again to defeat him.

Being encased in a dungeon beneath the birth city of his enemies was for Pitch a humiliation too loathsome to bear. And Big Root lived up to its name admirably. When Pitch was buried beneath the earth of the tree, its deep, sprawling roots braided into an elaborate, inescapable series of buttresses, and walls that fused with the metallic rock left by the meteor. This rock had given the tree its otherworldly power. In the passing centuries Ombric had learned that the meteor was made of what is called "dark matter," the only element in the universe that Pitch could not breach or break.

And so Pitch lay there in complete isolation. Weakened, silent, weary but waiting.

Nightlight. Jack Frost. Whatever name the boy had. Pitch would soon get his revenge upon him. He had set his plan in motion. It was a plan he had nurtured for decades. And now it was ready to be let loose.

CHAPTER FOUR

An Unusual Pair of Tails

DESPITE THE GUARDIANS' VALIANT efforts to isolate Pitch, there were creatures . . . beings . . . entities that walked the Earth in his service. Two in particular were eager to further their master's plans. Their identities—their very existences—was unknown to any of the Guardians. The Guardians had once been very familiar with them, fought them, even vanquished them. But that had been centuries ago, and these two had changed forms and shapes so that they were now completely unrecognizable. Thus, they moved outside the Guardians' detection.

These two were not specters or phantoms like Pitch's Nightmare Men, but were flesh and blood. They were men, at least of a sort—at close inspection it became apparent that there was something off about each. One had an abundance of legs, which he tried to hide under a long coat. There was also a fleeting glimpse of what appeared to be a thin hairy tail. The other fellow was rather doughy, with bulging eyes that gave his peculiar face a masklike expression of constant alarm. He also possessed a tail, a grotesque appendage of considerable girth and wormish looks.

Lampwick Iddock of the Many Legs was the more polished of the pair. He dressed elegantly and had what appeared to be a gracious manner. He was, in fact, polite to a fault. But like many creatures of prey, his pleasing outward appearance was merely a disguise, what Ombric would have called a "phasma,"

The phasma Lampwick and Blandim

which is a word of Greek origin with many expressive definitions: "a trick of the eye," "an apparition," or most colorfully, "the monster in a velvet cloak." Like the Venus flytrap, the pleasing scent of which could lure insects to their doom, Lampwick Iddock used his charm and demeanor to hide his brutal and murderous intent.

His companion—his sidekick in crime, his partner—was named simply Blandim. The name fit this oafish child-man to perfection. He was on the surface agreeable, if not a bit clueless. He appeared almost stupid. He smiled constantly and nodded incessantly and chuckled at Lampwick's every utterance. He seemed as bland and unthreatening as a Shetland pony, but he was at heart more conniving and cruel than even Lampwick.

These creatures had a long history with Pitch and

an even longer one with the Guardians. Iddock had once been an actual man, a maharaja who had once battled Queen Toothiana. But since coming under Pitch's power, both he and Blandim had displeased their master and had been turned into a series of ever-lowlier creatures. Pitch had promised to return them both back to human form if they succeeded in this new mission. The Nightmare King had managed to send instructions to these former associates. The two phasma were now well equipped by Pitch for the task he had assigned them. They knew exactly how to find, trap, and—with their master's further instruction— bring an end to the threat of Jack Frost's power.

CHAPTER FIVE

The Guardians Begin to Guard

THIS YEAR HAD BEEN one of particular unease for the Guardians.

Jack had kept to himself, which was his tendency under even normal circumstances. But this year he'd grown more distant. Since the establishment of the Earth Holidays, the Guardians had focused on their individual tasks, and their public identities had evolved. Their fame and influence had been smashing successes. They were known and revered the world over, and their devotion to guarding the spirit of Earth's children was unmatched in ambition and effect. They brought a genuine hope to the world. Not just for the young, but for those who held hard to the notion of remaining what was called "young at heart."

Sanderson Mansnoozie was now known simply as the Sandman. He not only used his Dreamsand to help children sleep when excited, afraid, or overstimulated, but he also dealt with the persistent battling of Pitch's remaining Nightmare troops, though this chore was one that every Guardian shared.

Queen Toothiana was generally referred to as the Tooth Fairy or simply Tooth. From her headquarters in Punjam Hy Loo, she oversaw the vast exchange of the lost teeth of Earth's children for various trinkets left under pillows. In her fortress stronghold she and her fairy armies catalogued and guarded these countless teeth and the childhood memories they contained.

E. Aster Bunnymund, the last of the tribe of giant rabbits called Pookas, was now known throughout the world as the Easter Bunny. It had been Jack himself who had suggested the reconfiguring of Bunnymund's first initial, E., and his middle name, Aster, into "Easter," as well as the delivering of eggs on that particular holiday Sunday in spring. This idea was, at first glance, a lark, but it quickly took hold. Chocolate eggs were Bunnymund's specialty, but soon actual eggs dyed a multitude of colors were added to the occasion, and the hiding of these eggs (again, Jack's suggestion) and their placement in baskets filled with grass evolved quickly. Bunnymund's already intricate underground tunnel-highways became even more elaborate and made the delivery of the eggs much more possible in a single evening.

North, too, made his Christmas Day

extravaganza with a similar all-in-one-night urgency and ingenuity, but now he made a point of always outdoing Bunnymund in scale and panache. Theirs was a friendly, joking rivalry, though Bunnymund never fully understood any joke. His Pookan mind had yet to grasp the idea of humor, though he tried.

It may seem that North's evolution into the being known as Santa Claus (the name came from Ombric's magic village of Santoff Claussen) had been the most dazzling of the Guardians' transformations, and in many ways that opinion was merited. Christmas had become more than a single day; it had become a state of mind that stretched out over an entire season. It became a distinct feeling. Though cloaked by winter, Christmas had an unmistakable warmth. The custom of decorated trees, colored lights, songs, presents, and a delirious variety of pageantry blended together to create this feeling. It was hopeful and comforting and slightly unreal, perhaps better than real, and it became known affectionately as Christmastime, a term that greatly pleased North and his former mentor, Ombric.

Of all the Guardians, Ombric Shalazar had been in some ways the most radically transformed. His valiant sacrifice during the Battle of Bright Night had been a dangerous gamble, and indeed it left him in a state that would have terrified a less experienced soul. He now barely existed at all, at least not in a form that science could explain. But Ombric's cumulative knowledge of magic, science, and time had left him with a different expectation of what would happen if he no longer existed as actual matter. He existed now as a being of time itself or, perhaps more accurately, in between time. He could move about through the past and present, but he was never really in either.

His beard pooled in great heaps around him and was so white, it was almost transparent. You were never sure when you might catch a glimpse of him, but he could communicate when he was called. And the Guardians called upon him often. Children had named him Father Time, and it was his ability to slow time that made the ventures of Christmas, Easter, and the Tooth Fairy possible. Only by bringing time to a near halt were North, Bunnymund, and Tooth able to accomplish their tasks in such short order.

How thoroughly Ombric controlled time was always something of a mystery, but this much they all assumed: Father Time could never venture into the future.

The Man in the Moon was now the gentle Zeus

of the Guardians' living mythology, and his word was undisputed law. Bunnymund, Mansnoozie, and Jack began as Golden Age creatures. North, Ombric, Katherine, and Tooth started life as human, or mostly so. But the Man in the Moon, or MiM, as the other Guardians sometimes called him, had been royalty of the Golden Age, and within his heart lived all that was worthy from that rare, majestic time.

Despite the murder of MiM's parents by Pitch, despite the tragedy of his orphaned life within the Moon, despite all the loss and loneliness he had endured, he had remained as kind in thought and deed as the most innocent of children. But he also had a great wisdom. He seldom ordered the Guardians to do anything. He instead guided them as a grandfather guides his grandchildren. And like all grandfathers, he was much stronger and more resilient than expected.

He had, after all, withstood trials that would fell even the mightiest.

Brave little Katherine had now grown up. Because of Kailash, Katherine was known throughout the world as Mother Goose. All of her famous stories and rhymes were based on incidents, beings, and creatures that were a part of her growing up with the Guardians. But her duties extended far beyond penning entertainments for children, for she also chronicled the history and goings-on of the Guardians, their many struggles and triumphs. These histories were not for the amusement of the outside world, but were instead intended for the Guardians themselves. Their lives had become so lengthy and rich that the Guardians sometimes needed or simply wanted to read and remember how things had once been. History, especially one's own, can sometimes help even a mighty Guardian understand the confusions of the present.

And these were indeed confusing times for the world and for the Guardians—1933 had been among the darkest years they had experienced in their Earthly dominion. A malady that grown-ups called the Great Depression had enshrouded the globe, and it affected virtually every man, woman, and child. The forces of upset were testing the Guardians' abilities and expertise. For all their knowledge of magic and potions and dreams and stories, for all their bravery and goodness, this Great Depression left the Guardians baffled.

It had begun with something called the Crash. But what exactly had crashed was almost impossible for them to grasp. They'd discussed it intently when its symptoms first appeared. "A market of some sort," explained Bunnymund. "Filled with socks, I believe."

"The word I heard was 'stock.' It was a market of stocks," corrected North.

"No, I'm sure it was socks, my bearded, bloated friend," replied Bunnymund. "I mean to say, what is a 'stock,' anyway? That makes no sense at all. The word is 'sock.' It was a sock crash!"

"Bunnymund, your ears may be large, but your brain is a molecule!" responded North. "Socks do not make a crashing sound when they fall, even in an impressive mound. They simply tumble, and having tumbled, they certainly couldn't make a crashing sound that could account for all the chaos that's happening now!"

It was a socioeconomic calamity encompassing the world economy, mused Sandy in his elegant, golden sandscript, which floated in the air above them. *A severe downturn in equity prices of commonly traded stocks in companies across all markets, causing a panic and an ensuing "crash" of stock prices.* The sleepy fellow paused. The explanation was so complicated, it had made him fall asleep.

"I mean, I know how the whole rigmarole happened," said North. "I just haven't a clue as to what it means."

"Indeed," Bunnymund remarked dryly. "These adult enterprises are not our strong suit."

And so the Guardians had watched with everdesperate alarm as millions of grown-ups lost their jobs, their homes, their farms, everything. Countless families now roamed the open road, desperate for a roof over their heads, a place to sleep, or even a hot meal. The Guardians saw this vividly during their gift-delivery efforts on this Christmas Eve.

Thousands of children could not be located. Many deliveries could not be made. The entire world seemed adrift. This hurt them. And where, oh where, was Jack Frost?

CHAPTER SIX

Misgivings on Giving Gifts

MOST YEARS, JACK'S DUTIES on Christmas Eve were primarily of his own choosing. He could fly on the wind to any place on Earth in a matter of minutes, and so he tended to keep a watchful eye on the entire undertaking. If there was a sudden, disastrous tangle of Toy Supply Balloon Blimps over Europe, he would drop in to sort out the traffic jam and send the blimps on to their assigned locations. Thus, as North and his sleigh made their way to each city, they could load up with the requested toys that were stored within these blimps and then blanket that city and its surrounding

towns and villages with the wished-for toys of the children who lived there. If time allowed, Jack would accompany North on some of his deliveries. The quiet, secretive nature of leaving the toys under trees and in stockings without being seen was pure joy, and something of a contest between the two. Being the fastest and the quietest was the goal, and Jack could not help but trick and tease his old friend.

That's the wrong present, he might say to North.

Don't try your tricks on me, runt. This is 1211 Pearly Pine Way. Little Tommy Gladstone. Aged seven. A drum set, toy soldiers, a bow and arrow, and a sailboat. It's all here on the Certified Deliveries List!

No, no, no, that's two houses down. This is Young Bertram and Louisa Ternwhistle. They asked for six actual ponies, two flying automobiles, and a real baby elephant!

What?!

Don't tell me you forgot the baby elephant.

That's ridiculous!

I guess you forgot flying automobiles, too?

North would then realize that Jack was kidding, and then they'd finish the real delivery. North would get his milk and cookies, and they'd both peek in at the sleeping children. Jack knew how almost every child's year had gone. And Santa knew which children Jack favored: the lonely and sometimes troubled ones. The ones Jack would purposefully erase from the final list of Naughties.

Every kid deserves a break or two, he'd tell North, *especially from a jolly fat man who's supposed to be the good guy.*

So says the naughtiest boy of all, North would reply with a chuckle, yet he always followed Jack's advice

on how to deal with a naughty or nice child.

This year, however, was different. North was alone. Jack was keeping his distance. His wounded hand throbbed with pain constantly; he felt sure that he was being followed. There were more Nightmare Men out there, or something like them. And he was certain that his being close to any Christmas deliveries would only bring trouble.

Even from a distance, Jack could see that this Christmas was not going well.

———◆———

CHAPTER SEVEN

A Yuletide Most Untidy

OUT OF CAUTION, JACK was waiting for the group back at the pole when the Christmas deliveries were completed. Katherine was relieved to see him, but the other Guardians could all tell from the look on Jack's face that he was even more worried than they were. North decided not to question Jack's absence. He knew the boy had been doing his best in his own way.

"I fear for what is to come," Tooth said, expressing what each of them was feeling. "The grown-ups are becoming desperate. The children are staying strong and steady, but all this uncertainty, this dread, takes its toll on them."

"Indeed," North agreed. "But I'm afraid worse things are in store."

"Another war?" asked Bunnymund. The mere mention of the word woke Sandy from his nap. Black sand began to curl about his head. They all remembered that awful war. The one called the World War.

"The grown-ups seem to be going crazy again," said Tooth. "Imagine becoming so angry and foolish that you would destroy homes, lands, lives!"

"Yes," said Bunnymund. "I'd rather hoped that grown-up humans would behave better than this."

But North had a different view. "I have to say I'm not surprised, just disappointed. I thought perhaps we would help children grow up in a way that would remind their adult selves what they know is wrong."

Toothiana twitched a wing. "I worry about something more. I worry that children will stop believing." The idea made them go quiet. Belief was the lifeblood of everything the Guardians hoped to achieve. To make children believe in the power of magic. To believe in the magic of the impossible.

Katherine had yet to say anything. Her relief at seeing Jack was tempered by a new concern. She had been watching as Jack silently paced at the edge of North's study. He was most close to the children, in temperament and form, so she knew these events were affecting him most of all. Her heart ached to see the strain on him.

And so they sat or paced and muddled over this Great Depression that threatened the world they loved so dearly. Then each became aware of the other having the exact same thought. Beginning in their earliest days together, they had developed the ability to share thoughts and feelings during times of crisis or great happiness. And this was a crisis that gave them each the same desperate thought: If only Ombric could use his powers to tell them the future, tell them how to fight the gloom that seemed to threaten the world.

The room suddenly illuminated, and the wizard's image flickered at the center. Ombric had heard them. He appeared as a strobelike phantom, desperate to tell them something. But they could not make out what he was trying to say—his voice was unclear, splintered. The massive efforts to slow time across all of Earth during Christmas had clearly wearied the wizard.

"Calm yourself," North gently said to his old teacher. "You have done all you can for now."

In response Ombric pounded his fists in the air, as if trying to break through from his twilight existence. He was like a madman in his desperation.

"He'll burn himself out!" cried Tooth.

"North," said Bunnymund, his voice uncommonly concerned for a Pooka, "you must calm him."

But before North could say more, Ombric slumped, shaking his head in exhaustion, his long beard sweeping against the floor. He began to fade. But as he did, he looked very deliberately at Jack Frost. Jack returned the gaze. Their exchange was intense, but Ombric's expression gradually grew serene. The furrows on his brow smoothed. Father Time and Jack were speaking with only their thoughts, but oddly, these thoughts were blocked from the other Guardians. They could feel a mental wall in their minds that kept this conversation from them, but it did not feel like an unfriendly act of secrecy. They trusted Ombric's judgment in speaking only to Jack. The old wizard always had a reason, and he had never failed them.

North mused, "He's helping us the only way he can."

Ombric grew dimmer still. His figure became as hazy as fog, but his eyes, fixed on Jack's, remained bright. Finally, Jack seemed to nod. Then Ombric blinked, and with that blink, he was gone.

Jack stared transfixed at the place Ombric had just left. He didn't seem aware that the others had quietly encircled him. It was Katherine who spoke first.

"Jack?" she said.

"How can we help, boy?" asked North. But Jack would not answer.

"We should call the Man in the Moon," Bunny-mund suggested.

"No!" shouted Jack, rousing at last. He took Katherine's hand and, gazing off into the distance, said, "I need one of your stories, Miss Goose. It's been a long time since you told me one."

And in an instant they were flying away from the North Pole on Kailash. The sky was a sea of stars, and Jack kept his eyes on the Moon, full above them. Katherine knew not to ask him any questions; he would speak when he was ready. To be with Jack, alone, was a rare gift these days. He was still holding her hand. Hers was warm. His was cold, so cold.

Though centuries had passed since they'd first met, in their hearts they were the same age again, the same as when they had first saved the world and each other.

The Moon was shining down on them as they rode through the night sky. They had been through so much together, and there was drama ahead. But tonight the warmth of their memories gave them the strength to face the troubles that were surely coming.

But for these brief hours they were Katherine and Nightlight once more.

CHAPTER EIGHT

The Everlasting Lip Touch

I*T ALL BEGAN WITH a kiss*, remembered Katherine as they flew. *That's when Nightlight ended and Jack Frost began.*

She thought back to the War of Dreams so many years ago, when Pitch had imprisoned her in an endless nightmare of sleep. Nightlight had guessed that a kiss would break that awful spell. But no one knew that this kiss would change them both forever.

Nightlight was a special being of the Golden Age. The Nightlights were a secretive brotherhood about which almost nothing was known. Ombric,

Bunnymund, even Nightlight himself knew very little about the brotherhood, and understood even less. Katherine was certain of only the following: Nightlight had existed for a single purpose: to protect one child. That child was young Prince Lunanoff, who became MiM, the Man in the Moon. Nightlight was also the last of his kind, and he was never intended to grow up. He was a childlike being, a celestial creature with vast powers. But a kiss is human magic, and when Nightlight kissed Katherine, the magic of the Golden Age and the magic of humans mixed and merged and made a new magic that was unlike any the universe had ever seen.

The kiss had only lasted a second or two. Ombric had measured it at exactly 2.86001 seconds, and Bunnymund referred to it as the "everlasting lip touch," which struck Katherine as a very Pookan way to describe what had happened. Ombric had tried to explain some of what their kiss had unleashed when he told them, "For humans, the first kiss is the end of childhood and the beginning of the grown-up journey. When two beings understand each other completely and never tire of each other, when they are always eager to be in the other's company, when they find delight even in the other's faults and trust in everything they do, when absence brings both anguish and strength, and when hope is made solid, then a kiss brings forth the most powerful magic of all. It creates an unshakable belief. Belief in another."

And so it was with Nightlight and Katherine. This kiss brought about an unshakable belief in the wonder and goodness of each other. And this belief became amplified by Nightlight's powers. In those 2.86001 seconds Pitch's Nightmare spell on

Katherine was shattered, and she awakened from her near-endless sleep, but in her heart she knew that something in both of them had been transformed. It would be a long time before they understood in full the extraordinary transformation, which was to come.

But instead of bringing them together, the kiss and its after-effects pulled them apart. Nightlight would vanish for more than a hundred years. And while Katherine never stopped believing that she'd see him again, his absence took its toll on her. She missed him. She missed their bond. She missed the brightness of his company.

Then, in the winter of 1890, she and the other Guardians began to hear tales of an untamed, white-haired youth who varied in age and made a mark on all who encountered him. His exploits quickly became legendary. He had taken on the identity of a dazzling young gentleman of great wit and zestful temperament named Jackson Overland Frost.

It was Katherine who first suspected that Jack Frost was Nightlight transformed. An article in the *London Times* described this young Mr. Frost, who had taken London by storm:

His handsomeness is pleasing in a way that crosses over into curiosity. He has a face that invites a second look. And then the urge to stare. His features seem to exist in some twilight between youth and adulthood. His skin has a slight iridescence, like a perfect layer of new-fallen snow in moonlight. His complexion is pale, but there is always a flush of red in his cheeks, setting off the icy blue of his eyes. His shock of white hair is like a crown of

mischief, a sort of proclamation of roguish royalty. Even at his most thoughtful, there is about him an air of cheerful possibilities, of pranks or fun about to be had—and in abundance. Reports of his age seem to vary. Some guess him to be in his early teens, while others are adamant that he is at least several seasons past twenty.

Upon reading this, Katherine knew in her bones that this Jack Frost must be Nightlight. The last time she had seen her friend, he radiated the same qualities and features, but it was the lack of certainty about his age that also stood out to her.

In the years after Nightlight had disappeared, Katherine aged as any young girl would, until she turned sixteen. Then something extraordinary happened. Whenever her thoughts dwelled on Nightlight, she would instantly become younger, usually around twelve years old, the precise age she had been when Nightlight had kissed her. She could remember everything that had happened to her since the kiss, but she was not only physically younger, she could also remember exactly what it *felt* like to be younger. The feelings and thoughts one has at twelve are different than at any other time of life. So in a strange way she could go back in time and remember and actually become her childhood self.

For years she kept this new ability a secret from the other Guardians. It, after all, happened only when she thought of Nightlight. It kept him vivid in her mind. There were many times when he seemed to be as close as a sigh, and this became a great comfort. His absence was a wound she kept to herself, so this tender marvel of remembrance felt very personal and private.

But in time it became obvious to her and the other Guardians that the kiss had changed her in other ways. By the time she was in her twenties, her aging slowed and then stopped completely.

After rigorous examination and much discussion the Guardians came to the conclusion that Katherine had changed from a mortal Earth child to a Golden Age woman who might very well live forever.

"Seldom has a kiss brought about such amazements," North had told her. "The history of the cosmos may likely be changed."

Katherine didn't know if that was true, but she did wonder what the kiss might have done to Nightlight. And when she heard these stories of Jack Frost, she felt sure that she at last had an answer. But it was as elusive as Jack Frost.

✦ ✦ ✦

By the 1890s the Guardians had organized an army of allies and observers that kept a helpful eye on children all over the world. North and Bunnymund spoke the languages of almost every creature on Earth, which made the gathering of information very thorough. Birds, mice, dogs, cats, squirrels, insects, and fish were privy to virtually every occurrence indoors and out, and so when Jack Frost appeared near the end of the century, his movements and secrets were communicated to the Guardians almost immediately.

The Guardians decided that this Jack Frost needed further observation. The reports on him were tantalizing.

He hardly sleeps! Sandy noted.

"He's at ballets, operas, art exhibits, and parties, seemingly all at the same time!" Bunnymund added.

North raised his formidable eyebrows and said,

"And what a jolly group of friends he has—magicians and jugglers, acrobats and clowns!"

"As well as novelists, poets, composers, artists, actors, playwrights, and even some politicians," Toothiana added. "He seems to have enchanted them all!"

Bunnymund twitched one ear and lowered his voice. "It's said that this Frost fellow has inspired stories and characters as varied as Dr. Jekyll and Mr. Hyde, Dorian Gray, and even Peter Pan!"

They call him "Wild Jack"! Sandy reported.

"Royalty seeks him out," Toothiana mused. "He's broken many hearts, and he seems to do the impossible daily: gallivanting in Moscow with Rasputin on a Friday evening and then attending the races at Ascot in England the following morning and not only riding the winning horse in the Gold Cup, but then presenting Queen Victoria the cup and giving her a lock of his cold white hair!"

North said in wonder, "Women adore him and men want to be like him."

And most important, the Guardians observed, was that children loved him.

No matter what glamorous bacchanal he was involved in, Jack always took the time to help any child who needed aid. If a child was hungry, cold, or without shelter, Jack made sure they were safe and comfortable. Tea at Buckingham Palace could wait, as could the queen. If Jack sensed a street child's sorrow, the queen would be left wondering where her luminous guest had gone. For beyond Jack's thirst for the whirl of experiencing life, there was a deep, unbending duty, or need, to take away the loneliness, the uncertainties, the fears of childhood and replace them with solace and comfort.

Jack did this quite simply.

He was kind and he listened.

He never, however, let a new friendship last for very long. His company was like that of a shooting star, a bright and wondrous flash, and then he would vanish. He wouldn't cut off a friend completely, but he would become aloof. Seldom seen. A pleasant phantom.

And of equal interest, it was found that he could also become invisible when he wished. He could fly great distances by a force that could not be seen. He was able to walk on clouds, and on the rare occasions when he did sleep, it was always during a full moon and on a drifting cloud. He had a staff that apparently wielded an assortment of extraordinary powers. Most important, he could, in fact, change his age at will, but never younger than eleven or older than eighteen.

Yes, thought Katherine at the time. *This must be my Nightlight. The kiss has given him the same ability as mine. But why has he not shown himself to us?*

It had been this question that had made the old wound of Nightlight's absence ache as if new. In her daydreams he had seemed so close and yet so far away. In reality, her plight was the same.

Then one extraordinary night in London their past caught up with their present.

CHAPTER NINE

Where There's a Will, There's a Whisper

As THEY NEARED THE Isle of Ganderly, where Katherine lived, she realized that Jack had fallen asleep against Kailash's feathers. He seemed so desperately to need rest. His brow was furrowed, making him seem older than he was. The many burdens of his long life weighed on him, she could tell.

As Kailash's powerful wings stilled into a glide, Katherine wished Jack was peaceful. But she knew he hadn't been, for a long, long time. As she watched him now, she thought back to the report of his last night in London. She had not read it in years, but when it had first come in, she had gone over it countless times, desperate for any news of her dearest friend. And now she could remember every detail.

Several mice, six doves, one finch, and a red squirrel had observed the events of that evening. They reported as follows:

It was a piercingly cold winter night. Jack was leaving the Athenaeum Club. He belongs to many clubs. Private clubs are a vital function of the social life of young and old men in this whirligig era. These clubs are elegant and brimming with friendships, rivalries, and the excitable friction of men with ambition and ideas. It is at the Athenaeum that Jack has

made some of his most interesting
friendships.

On the night of this report,
Frost was seen walking out of the
festive warmth of the club with three
companions. They were bundled against
the cold, laughing and chatting as
they trekked their way down the snow-
covered steps to the street. As is his
habit, Jack hung back a few paces. He
enjoys observing the easy joviality of
his friends at the end of an evening
of fun. The most affable of the three
is young Winston Leonard Spencer-
Churchill, whose booming laugh and
manner reminds Jack of his old friend
Nicholas St. North. Churchill had been

a devilish child, full of mischief,
and had been kicked out of most of
the finest schools in Europe. On this
evening he is smoking a huge cigar and
is at this point singing the song of
one of the schools he had attended.

"Sandhurst was a great school with
a wretched song!" he shouted out,
interrupting himself midchorus. The
other two friends, Joseph Rudyard
Kipling and James Matthew Barrie, are
both writers of some renown, though
tonight they were singing the song of
a school they had never attended and
were doing so with considerable volume
and enthusiasm.

"It would jolly well help if

we knew the words," said Kipling, laughing, but this ignorance did not seem to hamper his and Barrie's happy attempt.

Jack grinned. He liked his friends best when they behaved less like adults and more like children.

But as the group reached the sidewalk, they passed a huddle of street children who stood shivering in the evening air.

"Please, sirs, a penny for the hungry," said one child with a practiced, hopeful desperation.

Jack's friends did not even glance the children's way. These children were cold and close to starving. Jack

saw the ragged clothes. The thin,
lanky legs and skinned elbows. Again
Jack stayed back, watching as his
friends continued down the street.

The children stood quiet and
shivering. They watched the happy
threesome stagger and wail down the
street.

Jack appeared angry with his
friends. He knew they may have had
childhoods of comfort, but each had
experienced great turbulence and
heartbreak in their youths. They should
not, could not, would not ignore the
wretched children they had just passed.
They must be made to listen.

So Jack made himself invisible. It

is a power he uses subtly. If a party
is dull, he will simply disappear.
Or if he wants to secretly influence
the outcome of an event, being unseen
makes his efforts much easier.

At this point in the proceedings
he discreetly launched three expertly
constructed snowballs at his friends.

Each hit its mark.

All three men's hats were knocked
to the snowy ground. The three
then spun around and stared at the
children. The children stared back.

Apparently, a war had silently been
declared.

"This aggression must not go
unanswered," muttered Churchill as he,
Kipling, and Barrie crouched down and

began busily packing snowballs.

Though invisible, we surmise that
Jack was delighted. He whispered
to various children, "Better get
busy. They're bigger than you." They
instantly fell to their knees and
began to pack snowballs themselves.

Churchill and Kipling both have
military histories and have seen
battle, so they knew the necessity of a
steady supply of ammunition. Barrie, as
records show, is the worst shot of the
three, so he continued making snowballs
while his cohorts took up positions
behind a lamppost and a mailbox.

"Wait for my command," said
Churchill, puffing his cigar.

The children were seasoned snowball

makers, and they had amassed an
impressive hoard of ammo. They were
ready to attack, but they seemed
uncertain. Again Jack intervened.
"Concentrate on the one with the
cigar."

The children were so focused on
their enemy that they hadn't even
noticed that Jack was nowhere to be
seen. They heard his suggestion, and
without questioning it, they acted.

And charged! Their battle cry was
high, shrill, and impressive. Eight
little voices sounded like an army.

"My word," said Kipling,
astonished.

"Steady!" commanded Churchill.

Barrie stopped his constructions and readied for the attack, a snowball in each hand and several in each pocket.

In an instant the children were upon them. The air was thick with snowballs and shouting and cheers.

"Fire!" yelled Churchill, but his command was muffled by five or six direct hits on his head and shoulders. He fell backward and lay on the street as helpless as an overturned turtle. Four children stood over him and pounded him with snowballs.

"My cigar!" he yelped. And indeed his cigar had been knocked from his mouth, landing somewhere inside his coat.

Kipling and Barrie tried to lend

aid, but both were hit with such accuracy that their eyeglasses were caked with thick clumps of snow and neither could see a thing.

The three men were being overwhelmed, routed, in fact. But suddenly, the tide of the battle changed. Twenty or so members of the Athenaeum Club had seen the skirmish from the windows and were rushing out to lend a hand.

Jack had reappeared and raised his staff, and within an instant, he brought about a blinding gale of snow to slow the Athenaeum men.

A smallish boy who looked particularly ragged raised two fingers to his mouth and let out a high, sharp whistle that could be heard for blocks. The boy had not finished his first note when children began to appear from seemingly every direction and swarm toward the fray.

And so this snowball battle became epic. Adults against children. Jack watched with astonishment. What had he triggered?

Old men—older than eighty—who minutes before could barely hobble with canes across a plush dining room carpet, were now rippling over snow-covered cobblestones with the vigor and skill of Roman gladiators.

Gangly half-starved children, some as young as five years old, were

standing their ground or attacking
with the stalwart cunning of the most
seasoned generals.

The blur of a thousand snowballs
glistened in the streetlamps' glow as
cheers and laughter of pure exultant
joy filled the air. The strange
untethered glee of making pretend war
with well-packed snow had turned men
into boys, and children into heroes.

Jack returned to invisibility, but
he stayed in the thick of this battle
royal, flying from place to place
faster than any snowball. He was heard
shouting instructions or guidance to
anyone he felt was in need. At first
he only helped the children, but as

the ruckus continued, he began to urge the Athenaeums on.

So focused were the combatants that none ever wondered who was helping them.

The fight reached a pitch so fevered that one by one participants began to collapse with exhaustion and merriment. There were calls of:

"Stop! Enough!"

"I surrender!"

"I'm done!"

Shouts became laughter. The din of the battle dissolved into a singsong of helpless giggling and gasping and guffaws.

Churchill struggled to his feet.

He was laughing with more gusto than anyone. He pulled his still-lit cigar from some deep fold of his coat and took a long and satisfying puff.

"I suggest we call an end to these hostilities," he said to the spent troops. "I suggest we call this battle a draw." He took another puff.

The half-block heap of young and old sat panting, their warm breath making a wheezing fog around them.

"I say we are all victors, and so to all must go the spoils," Churchill continued. "Let us retire to the warmth of the club. I urge that we leave the snow to fall in peace and that we feast like kings!"

Cheers of agreement rang out. As
they helped one another to their feet,
Churchill began again to sing his old
school song, the song of his beloved
Sandhurst:

> *"And so from those who have*
> *gone before, to those who are*
> *yet to come,*

> *We pass our motto loud and*
> *clear, all evil overcome.*
> *As true as is a brother's*
> *love, as close as ivy grows,*

> *We'll stand four square*
> *through our lives to every*
> *wind that blows."*

It was then that Frost tactfully reappeared as stealthily as he'd vanished in the first place. Smiling, he watched the scene unfold. Churchill slapped him on the back, still in full-throated song and joined by all who knew the words.

"They never saw me," Frost whispered to Twiner. "But I believe they thought I was there—" Then Jack froze midthought. His left hand (upon which there is a deep scar) suddenly clenched, as if in pain. As the others went inside past the great oak doors of the Atheneaum Club, Jack stepped aside and peered into the shadows of a nearby side street.

The Nightmare Men finally find Jack

It took a moment before the
Nightmare Men showed themselves.

In less than an instant Jack once
again turned invisible.

report 66g37* London

And as Katherine recalled, by dawn Jack had left
London and made his way to the North Pole. He had
returned to them, but in all the years since he had
never offered any explanation for his long absence or
why he was now called Jack Frost.

Katherine knew that Jack was hiding some dark
truth. And he was hiding it for a reason. She hoped
that now, perhaps, she would finally learn the secrets
of her fair-haired boy.

CHAPTER TEN

What's Good for the Goose
Is Grand for the Ganderly

KAILASH LIFTED ONE WING ever so slightly and
banked left, gliding silently toward Katherine's island,
to the topmost spire of the main house. It is difficult
to ascribe a structure as unique as Ganderly's as any
particular sort of building. It was larger than a house,
but not really a mansion. It had several towers, but it
wasn't a castle. It was beautiful, in some ways rather
grand, but it was by no means a palace.

It was rambling yet intimate. It was handsome
and sturdy, but also airy and graceful. It was certainly
elaborate, but in a simple, uncluttered way. There were

porches and balconies and decks and walkways and roofs; some were peaked and pitched and pointed. Others were rounded or flat.

But Ganderly's most notable feature was the half dozen or so massive trees that twined and curved their way around and throughout the house itself. These were saplings of Big Root, and they had the same gnarled sycamore bark of their mother tree, as well as flowing clusters of thick, elegant limbs that curled outside the windows and balconies. These limbs served as willowy paths and stairways upon which one could walk up to other windows or floors or simply sit amid the treetops that arched over the house like giant leafy umbrellas.

This unusual feature gave Ganderly the appearance of being a sort of tree house estate, which had been Katherine's plan from the beginning. As a child her favorite secret place had been the makeshift tree house she had made as a nest for Kailash in the topmost branches of Big Root. It was in that tree house that she began to write her many stories, where she first discovered that they had the power to help her make sense of the wonders and sorrows of the real world.

Ganderly had become her grown-up version of that hideaway, the place where, as Mother Goose, she lived and thought and dreamed and wrote. But tonight she would not write. Tonight Jack needed a story. A story to help him make sense of whatever it was that Ombric had told him. And hopefully, save them all.

But first he would need to wake up.

CHAPTER ELEVEN

How to Get the Goose

KAILASH SETTLED INTO HER gargantuan nest nooked in the balcony outside Katherine's quarters. Jack stirred.

"Did you dream?" Katherine asked him.

"Yes," he said, shaking off his sleepiness. "I had a dream of you." He said this in a way that flooded her with memories. He sounded as though he were trying not to be sad.

Katherine turned and smoothed Kailash's feathers, as was her custom after a journey. Jack scratched behind Kailash's ear with the tip of his staff. One of

Twiner's many powers was the soothing effect his scratch had on all great beasts: It brought indescribable peace to whoever's ear was being scratched. For the tribe of North Pole Yetis, the ear scratch was a very effective method of persuasion, especially among the full-blown giants called the Titans. These Titan Yeti roamed the outer perimeters of the North Pole, ever watchful for intruders or explorers. If anyone with evil intent neared the secret city of the north, the Titans would do what needed doing to protect it. With doers of evil, the Titans were generally merciless, but with explorers, they were more considerate. With the North Wind's help, they would fan up a blinding snowstorm to block any view of the North Pole. Sometimes the Titans would break off vast hunks of iceberg that caused explorers to float out into the Arctic Sea. When that "game" grew tedious for the Titans,

The power of the essential ear scratch

they fooled the next groups of explorers by creating a sort of phantom North Pole far from the sight of the actual city of wonders. This had been Jack's idea. He knew that explorers were searching for something that was scientific, factual, magnetic. Something that was at the geographical top of the world.

"Toys, magic, and Santa Claus are the last things on these learned gents' minds," Jack had informed the other concerned Guardians. "So I'll give them exactly what they're looking for, and then some." He'd then directed the Yetis to bury a number of large meteorites (which are extremely magnetic) to establish a "pretend" magnetic pole (all compasses point to this pole) and had the Yetis shift the ancient ice pack under North's city so that it was never anywhere near the magnetic or geographical top of the world.

Jack, however, couldn't resist yet another mischievous streak. He allowed several explorers, including the famous Admiral Robert Peary, a glimpse of the great city. He was certain that the adult world would never believe any discovery so fantastic. And indeed he was correct. Peary and his team were laughed at by scientists for claiming to have seen a great, glittering land always out of reach. Their sighting was dismissed as a mere mirage.

Jack understood the limits of the adult imagination as well as he understood the open minds of children and the secret weaknesses of Yetis. While the Titan Yetis were unquestionably heroic and strong, they could sometimes be difficult to corral into action. Lifting meteors and moving cities involved a bit of enticement. So Jack would scratch behind their bed-size ears with the crook of Twiner, and the Yeti Titans would do anything Jack asked.

And so it was also with Kailash. The great goose leaned into the gentle scuffing of the staff's tip at that perfect spot between head and nape. Himalayan Snow Geese are notoriously aloof to those outside of their daily experience, but Kailash had always been partial to a good ear scratch and gave a sort of slow, goosey, gurgling, giggling sigh.

Glancing toward a window, Jack made sure that Katherine was inside the house before he leaned close and whispered, "Is Katherine happy?"

Kailash stopped her funny sigh and fluttered her eyes open. That was all Jack needed. He spoke fluent goose. The bird gurgled on.

Katherine is not unhappy. But neither is she happy, he gleaned from the goose. *But she is very "bright" to see Jack.*

"Bright" was a very goosian choice of words. Geese

think in simple terms, and bright was always a good thing. Bright was like sunlight or something shiny. To geese, it meant "pleased" or "lucky" or "tickled," all words that Jack liked to hear. In his long absences he missed Katherine and worried about her, though he hated to admit it.

He sometimes wished for the simpler time when he had been Nightlight. When he was a Nightlight, his feelings were pure, uncluttered, like those of a child. But that was more than a century ago, and there was no way to go back. He was Jack Frost now and would be forever.

And what he needed this night was an answer to what Ombric had put to him. He didn't understand what had been asked of him, and he was hoping Katherine could help.

CHAPTER TWELVE

The Greatest Library the World Has Never Known

THE NUMBER OF BOOKS IN Ganderly was beyond impressive. Within its many rooms, thousands of shelves pressed snugly upon one another with an ever-growing mass of volumes. Katherine's *Rhymes and Tales*, the works we call Mother Goose stories, were but a tiny fraction of her collection. As dowager empress of stories, her library contained virtually every book devoted to children that had ever been. They spread throughout Ganderly in alphabetical order, and far beyond Ganderly as well: Katherine functioned under many guises and disguises to establish libraries and sections of libraries that were devoted to children's books all over the world.

She was aided in this endless endeavor by the citizens of a tiny nation-state not far from Istanbul (formerly Constantinople) located on the Bosporus Strait. The name of this land was Raconteuristan, and its people were called Raconturks. For millennia, the rulers of Raconteuristan had been chosen not by birth or by lineage or by who was most cunning or adept at war, but by the beauty, wit, and power of the stories they told. Theirs was a nation of the imagination, with a history that mixed fact and fiction with joyful abandon. Entire eras and epochal events may or may not have happened. If the myth sounded good and was entertaining, then it was proclaimed true. The only rule the Raconturks insisted upon was that no fiction could be used to hurt any real person, and most important, anyone who was overtly cruel or mean would be banished. The Raconturks' history had many

A Raconturk

villains, none of them actual, and an endless series of heroes who may or may not have existed. So when the Raconturks became aware of Katherine, or rather Mother Goose, they felt as if the most wonderful story of all had at last come true. They called her Lady Goose.

The Raconturks volunteered to be Katherine's secret army and proved themselves to be invaluable as unofficial diplomats in the service of spreading the importance of stories. In every town, village, city, and hamlet, they posed as teachers, professors, and scholars, but most often librarians, devoting their lives to inspiring people, especially children, to not only read, but also to *write*. In time the notion of growing up and being a writer began to take hold as a genuine possibility for thousands of imaginative people. And this was the beginning of one of the most powerful and important forces of the Guardians: an actual protective field that encircled the entire Earth.

The Man in the Moon called it the Mythosphere, and from it coursed an invisible layer of enchantment that could inspire any man, woman, or child who needed or desired to tell a story. This had been Katherine's inspiration. She had discovered during her childhood with Ombric that stories could save people. They had helped her save North when he nearly died of his wounds protecting the children of Santoff Claussen. And they had saved her, transforming her from a shy, lonely, seemingly powerless orphan into a being who, even as a child, could stand toe-to-toe with the most potent villain in the cosmos, Pitch himself.

Pitch was keenly aware of Katherine's growing influence. He had always known that Katherine would develop into a formidable entity. That had been the primary reason why he had tried to convert her into becoming his Darkling Princess, why he had submerged her into that dark sleep when she had resisted, the sleep that Nightlight had woken her from with that single kiss. And now, even in *his* deep isolation, Pitch felt the shift in Katherine's growing powers.

But this new component of the Guardians' defenses, these ever-amassing stories, struck some deep and fearful alarm inside his dark heart. Spells, magic, jolliness, chocolate eggs, presents, elves, teeth—all the Guardians' methods to fight his darkness were, to him, puny parlor tricks. But this power of story? He could not figure out how to fight a story.

"A cow jumps over the Moon. A boy named Huck saves his friend," he would rant to himself. "Things that never actually happened! And yet they *matter*. They *move* people. Make them *care*. They give them escape. They give them hope. They make them less afraid!" He simmered with the rage of the ignorant. "How do I fight something that isn't *real?*"

For more than a century he'd puzzled over this. As with most mysteries, when the solution came, it was simple. The clean, elegant cruelty of the scheme he was devising became vital to him. It delighted him. He lay in his prison, concocting his *own* story, a story of revenge. And this story had indeed saved him in a way. Changed him. Made him even craftier. This plan gave him new life and purpose. And for the first time he understood the power he was fighting. But his story would not be used to help or heal.

This story was everything the Raconturks fought against.

This story would cause hurt. It would *destroy.*

CHAPTER THIRTEEN

In Which We Get to the Root of the Matter

Jack Frost's many homes were scattered evenly across Earth, all of them inside the hollows of large trees. Each was the offspring of Big Root, and these "children" of Big Root were often the oldest tree in the forest where they grew. They had all been planted soon after Bright Night by Twiner. Twiner himself came from a willow called Warrior's Willow, which stood on ancient Viking burial grounds. From its branches Viking warriors and hunters fashioned the strongest and most flexible bows, staffs, and arrows. The warrior dead were buried among the willow's

roots, and each limb was said to have the spirit of a warrior within its heartwood. This spirit could help the person who wielded it, but only if that person were brave and true of heart. Jack's staff was his friend, his comrade, his protector. It would alert him to danger. It could focus Jack's power to speak to the wind and learn the language of leaves.

On this particular day, in a forest near the Isle of Ganderly, the trees saw something that worried them. Two men were making their way toward Mother Goose's home. The trees of many lands had been watching these two since they had begun their journey from the jungle of Punjam Hy Loo. But the trees had waited to send out warning to any Guardian until they felt a genuine threat.

These two men traveled by car or train or boat when necessary, but they preferred to travel by tree, swinging from branch to branch when possible. Thus, the trees discovered what these men had once been, and now knew they meant ill. They knew that Twiner must be sent an urgent message: *An old enemy is near!*

CHAPTER FOURTEEN

Anger Management

ODDLY ENOUGH, THE RACONTURKS were fiercely effective guards of Ganderly. Being well read, they had studied every kind of close-quarters combat and had made up several of their own, all of them derivations of ninja, kung fu, Shaolin, and classic fisticuffs, incorporating sabers, swords, clubs, and even a method of using books as shields or like boomerangs. Most impressively, they had also contrived a method of using invented words that, when spoken at the proper volume and inflection, could completely incapacitate any foe. These words were called "onomatopoeia," and they were most impressive in sound and effect. *Fwapp! Kapow! Shhhing! Splat! Ka-ping! Ka-thunk! Crack-a-twang! Kerrrr-BLOOOM! Ker-SPLAT! KER-BLAM! KER-FWANG!* These words had been designed and tested for their power by the MOWS, the Mystic Order of the Word Smythes, who were a much-respected fraternal/maternal group within the Raconturks. Members of the MOWS made up the majority of Ganderly's guards.

The MOWS were on high alert with the arrival of Jack Frost at Ganderly. It had been a long time since there had been a visit from "The Jack," as they called him, and his arrival always brought an air of excitement and expectation. Jack was a great warrior and a kindred spirit. They admired him, and on those rare occasions when he visited, they were especially watchful, not only because Jack had about him an air of cheerful danger and had many enemies, but he was also known to trick them with humorous pretend attacks and other mischief.

Jack, however, was not in a mischievous frame of mind right now. He was quiet and intent. As Katherine led him to the deep inner chamber of Ganderly where the histories of the Guardians were kept, he barely glanced at the pair of guards who flanked the heavy bookshelf-covered doors. The guards sensed that this visit was different.

As they stood at attention, they discreetly peered inside the room, watching as Jack leaned Twiner against a wall of books. As the doors began to shut, the guards saw a large book fly down from the stacks. Their lady raised her arm, and the book landed lightly on her wrist, like a bird. They knew this volume well. It was the most important book in their lady's collection. It was Mr. Qwerty, the living book of all knowledge.

Mr. Qwerty had once been a bookworm of some note in Ombric's incomparable library. Pitch had once planned to steal Ombric's many volumes, and to thwart him, this valiant worm had consumed the entire collection. He actually ate every page of each individual book. This Herculean effort had kept Pitch from amassing the vast knowledge of the ages, including the great secrets of the lost civilization of Atlantis, all of which he had intended to use for evil.

For Mr. Qwerty, there were profound side effects. He immediately built his cocoon and emerged, weeks later, as a sort of butterfly book whose many wings were pages that could display the writings on any particular subject he had consumed. And Mr. Qwerty kept current. Katherine fed him copies of every

Mr. Qwerty—gentleman, worm, scholar, and book

book written since his remarkable evolution while making sure that he gobbled up a steady diet of all the Guardians' histories and adventures. So Qwerty, a former worm, became, in effect, the most important book in the history of knowledge and literature.

Now, Mr. Qwerty looked at them expectantly. Katherine was equally curious—in fact, she was near shivering in anticipation. Jack had wanted a story. They were among them all! Which would he choose? She turned to Jack. His eyes were bright.

"What story do you want to hear?" Katherine asked.

"One of mine," he said immediately.

Looking to the bookworm on her arm, Katherine said, "Mr. Qwerty, if you please, turn to the stories and adventures of the being called Nightlight now known as Jackson Overland Frost."

Mr. Qwerty's pages fluttered. The anticipated text appeared, and Katherine looked back at Jack. Then she asked the question that had been on her mind since Ombric had appeared to them earlier at the North Pole. "Is it a *story* that Ombric asked you about?"

Jack didn't answer immediately. He generally enjoyed being cleverly teasing in his conversations, but with Katherine, he was usually more direct and honest. Honesty is harder than being clever, and it often takes longer, too. As Katherine waited, she felt the entirety of their long relationship pass by in a matter of a dozen sated seconds. She was aging backward . . . growing younger, and so was Jack, until they became the age they were when they had shared that single kiss. This magic shift always startled them. They felt so young and yet so old.

"I'm not sure *what* he wants of me, Katherine,"

Jack said, starting to pace. Katherine understood why he wasn't sure. Ombric, like all good wizards, would seldom answer an important question directly. Instead, he would usually tell you just enough so that you could, after thinking through the situation, find the answer for yourself.

"All he said," Jack added with a knowing grin, aging himself from twelve to sixteen, "was 'Remember.'"

"Remember?"

"Remember."

Katherine shook her head with exasperation. "The world is in chaos and we ask for guidance, and all Father Time will allow us is one word?"

"Yep," said Jack. "Though it does have three syllables."

Mr. Qwerty snickered at that.

Katherine pursed her lips and tried to stay calm,

but she glowed with irritation. She sometimes grew impatient with the "figure it out yourself" logic of wizards.

"Can't I for *once* get a straight answer to a simple question?" she fumed. "A simple 'yes' or 'no' or 'here's what you do' would save so much time!"

Jack watched her, bemused. He had always admired her temper. And her ability to control it, or at least channel it into constructive action. Her fury could be prodigious at times, but she used it well and to great effect, like Zeus hurling thunderbolts. He honestly could not remember her ever completely losing her temper.

That said, memory had become a most curious element of his life since becoming Jack Frost. He found that he could erase the memory of entire sections of his life if he chose. And he often did.

Katherine, however, disliked this ability of his,

and she made no secret of it. For she now knew his life better than he did. Which felt wrong to her. *How will he ever be a real person, a whole person, if he simply erases the bad?* she often wondered.

She turned her fierce gaze to Jack. "So what exactly am I supposed to 'remember' for you?" She said this less as a question than an accusation, and her irritation began to transform her back into Mother Goose. As she grew older, taller, Jack had to fight the urge to run and hide like a child. And as she grew older, taller, he actually began to grow younger.

"I don't know," he said as he became one year younger.

"I see," she said curtly. He became one year younger still.

After an uncomfortable silence he made a suggestion he knew would irritate her even further.

"Katherine . . ." He shrank another year. "I trust you"—another year vanished—"to know best." He'd reached bottom. He could be shamed into growing no younger, and she could appear no older. He was back to twelve and she was twenty-five. There was a limit to how young he could transform. And he had reached it. He sat on the floor in front of the fireplace, his legs crossed, his back slumped. His head hung low.

"I can't wait to forget this," he remarked.

Katherine sighed. Though they were inches apart, the distance between them felt vast. She wished she could forget this, too, but she knew that was not the nature of things, at least for her.

For all the dash and glamour that being Jack Frost implied, Katherine knew the price he paid for his eternal youth. He had defeated Pitch more decisively than all the other Guardians combined. And he had done so with a selflessness and courage that had surprised even the Man in the Moon.

Now, yet again, the balance of the Earth's happiness or misery rested on his slender shoulders. It was in truth a terrible burden. One that no other Guardian had ever carried. And they sometimes forgot this, as adults often do. They forget how strong, how brave a child must be to live in the world of grown-ups. But Jack could never forget, for he was forever young. This is what set him apart from the other Guardians. It set him apart from every other being in the world.

Katherine sank to her knees in front of Jack. Mr. Qwerty fluttered and hovered above her as she smoothed the dark velvet skirt that she wore in winter. She looked to Jack. His gaze seemed far away, as if looking at a night sky devoid of stars.

He is making his mind blank, she realized, *and ready for what he will hear.*

So she shifted her gaze to Mr. Qwerty and nodded. The book came to rest in her lap. It was still open to the same page: the beginning of Jack's story. Katherine traced her fingers lightly over the paper as if feeling the words written upon them. The whole of Jack's life played out in her thoughts while the pages of Mr. Qwerty turned, grazing her fingertips as if blown by an unhurried wind. Back and forth, like cards in a shuffling deck, the pages fluttered, going forward and backward in Jack's history. So many adventures. So much joy and exhilaration and sometimes so much loneliness and sorrow. Jack's life was literally in her hands.

Which story does he need to hear? To remember? What happened in his past that can help him, help us all, to steady these dark days? Katherine focused every avenue of her mind on this single question. The pages riffled past her fingertips faster, and faster still, until a turbulent breeze began to roil about the room. Twiner began to rattle and shake against the wall.

And then the atmosphere intensified.

A noticeable charge filled the air.

It was the other Guardians. They had felt Katherine's concentration. And as they had so many times before, their minds joined. North, Toothiana, Bunnymund, Sandy, then the Man in the Moon himself. Even Mother Nature became a part of this effort.

From each of their headquarters on the Moon and across the Earth, their minds searched and probed Jack's history until the pages of Mr. Qwerty became a blur too fast to measure and the wind in the room grew to almost a gale. The fire in the hearth flickered and dimmed as it struggled to stay lit. Twiner was pulled into the maelstrom, caught in the whipping winds, but Jack seemed fully nonplussed—he extended one arm and snatched the staff down with a single effortless grab.

Then Katherine began to transform once more. Her features blended and smoothed. Years dissolved. The wind slowed. She again became the Katherine of her time with Nightlight. The pages eased their shuffling and stopped at last.

The mystery would unfold now. And each of them would be privy to its discovery.

But there was one more who would hear. One who was not meant to.

Deep under the Earth, the impossible occurred. In his prison Pitch, King of Nightmares, was listening to every utterance and syllable of the one story that could help him destroy the Guardians forever. And this eavesdropping was known only to Pitch—or was it?

Her girlish voice steady and clear, Katherine began to read from the history of Jack Frost:

THE STORY OF THE KISS

During the War of Dreams, before the Battle of Bright Night, Pitch had imprisoned Katherine on Nightmare Rock, the ancient stone that had once been his prison and was permeated to its core with all of Pitch's rage and hate. The rage had surrounded Katherine and created a shield that would keep anyone from ever waking her. He cast her into an endless sleep of nightmares with the hope that he would darken her soul, turn her to evil. Then he would make her his Darkling Daughter, his Princess of Nightmares.

But Nightlight and the Sandman found the cave where Pitch had entombed Katherine. They stole away the wretched rock and with Sandy's Dreamsand, levitated it to the North Pole. There, they and the other Guardians would try to break the Nightmare spell and free Katherine. But the rock was dense with countless Nightmare Men. As Sandy and Nightlight floated over the pole, the Nightmares began to charge from the stone and attack. All had seemed lost.

Then Nightlight remembered the power of the good night kiss. He remembered that the Man in the Moon's parents would kiss the baby MiM good night every night. He remembered that this kiss would take away all the hurt of the day. Nightlight then thought his most un-Nightlight-like thought. He knew a kiss was a powerful thing, a thing of hope, and he knew that he was a creature of unending hope, so his kiss must have great power. And he also knew something no Nightlight had ever known: that he loved. He loved his Katherine more than anything in all the universe. And though he did not even know how to give a kiss, he closed his eyes and lunged face-forward toward Katherine. The Nightmare shield gave way like vapor. And for an eternal instant Nightlight's lips touched

Katherine's, and all Pitch's dark spells withered away. Her eyes opened and Nightlight took her hand and together they flew to safety.

Nightmare Rock fell and landed harmlessly just beside the North Pole. The whole of the great city cheered and celebrated Katherine's rescue, and Nightlight was proclaimed a hero. The Sandman was made a Guardian.

And there was no sign of Pitch.

That night, after much merrymaking and ballyhoo, Nightlight and Katherine fell asleep in the topmost room of the pole. For Nightlight, it was a miraculous sleep, for he had never before slept. No Nightlight ever had. Nightlight was exactly what he was called: a light against the night. But now he was changed. The kiss had changed him forever. And though he had protected dreams for his entire life, he had never had one.

That night, he dreamt.

But Pitch did not. He had, in fact, tricked them all. He knew that North's magnificent tower was also a ship, a craft that could journey to the Moon.

The "North Pole," as it was called, was the tallest structure in the city. Its outward appearance was that of a curious sort of tower, but at its base were a number of engines that enabled the pole to rocket outside the Earth's atmosphere. North had intended his new craft to act as a sort of "space shuttle" to the Moon and back. The hope being that constant travel to the Moon would be not only jolly and inspiring, but also forge a closer bond with the Man in the Moon.

Ever since his grounding on Earth, Pitch had never been powerful enough to leave it. This craft,

The actual North Pole

this North Pole, was exactly what Pitch needed to complete his plan to destroy Nightlight. With the Guardians helplessly stranded on Earth, Pitch could extinguish Nightlight, conquer the Moon, and use it as his base to once again terrorize the galaxies. So he had hidden himself inside Nightmare Rock. He had successfully anticipated that the Guardians would bring the rock to the North Pole in an effort to save Katherine. He let them think they had defeated the Nightmare Men and rescued her. The next step in his plan was to kidnap Nightlight and fly the pole to the Moon. But luckily for Pitch, Nightlight was already asleep in the pole, as was Katherine.

Once the city had grown quiet, Pitch crept from the rock. Dragging it into the pole, he then found the control room and piloted the craft across the sea of space toward the Moon. As Pitch neared MiM's home, he used Nightmare Rock once more. Passing over the Moon's Dark Side, he launched the stone like a meteor and rode it as it fell. It crashed in the deepest crater on the darkest part of the Moon's Shadowlands, and with it, Pitch began to build his new Nightmare Army.

Nightlight and Katherine knew nothing of all this intrigue. They slept. And when the pole landed, they awoke, they were greeted by MiM himself, and there was much excitement and concern. MiM knew that something extraordinary had happened to Nightlight and Katherine. He also knew that Pitch would be—must be—planning a terrible revenge.

Katherine stopped her reading and glanced at Jack. He still sat cross-legged, staring into the fire. He held his staff in one hand, balancing its base on the floor. The diamond dagger tucked into his waistband glinted. Katherine's eyes narrowed. Jack had carried a diamond dagger in the old days, but this one was different. It was darker and seemed . . . strange.

She waited to see if Jack wanted her to read on. The next section of the story she had penned herself. It was from the sketchbook diary she'd kept in those long-ago days. But she'd always been uncomfortable reading her own prose aloud, so she was hesitant to continue. Especially now that it was about Jack, and he was the one who was listening. Finally, he nodded to her.

"Your voice always soothes me, Katherine," he said as if reading her mind, which was quite likely.

She thought how much he had changed since she'd written the entry she was about to read. He spoke with such elegance and confidence now, with only an occasional trace of the simple syntax of his Nightlight years.

She slipped back into the cadences of a born storyteller and began to read. If only she had known about the danger that was making its stealthy way across the grounds of the Isle of Ganderly. Jack seemed to be listening intently as she began. What she hadn't noticed was that he had moved his free hand down to the hilt of his diamond dagger and was gripping it with all his might.

Moon Days
From the Journal
of Katherine
While on the Moon

Nightlight had slept. I didn't understand the full wonder of this until after I awakened. I was doubly dumbfounded to find that we had traveled to the Moon in North's marvelous North Pole contraption. But who had guided the craft on this surprise journey was a mystery that compounded the oddness of suddenly discovering myself on the Moon for the first time.

"How long has Nightlight slept?" was the question that roused me from the deepest, most peaceful rest I'd ever known. I recognized the voice. I'd heard it several times before when we Guardians had managed with various devices to communicate with the Man in the Moon. But I'd never heard it so clearly or seemingly so close. That clarity is what jarred me awake to the astonishing sight of the Great Man Himself looking down at me. Trying not to be intimidated (hundreds of Moonbots, Moonmice, and a goodly number of glowworms and Lunar Moths peered down at me as well), I answered the question with the sum total of what I knew to be certain:

"I have no idea," I said.

This brought forth a blur of commotions, inquiries, exclamations, and whispered goings-on from which I gleaned this list of facts:

1. Nightlights are created
   from starlight, the laughs of
   ten thousand children, and
   a lock of hair from both
   a king and a queen of the
   Lunanoff family.

2. There have been only
   seven other Nightlights
   in all of history.

3. Nightlights transform into
   stars when the prince or
   princess they were created
   to protect grow up or no
   longer need protection
   from bad dreams.

4. Our Nightlight is
   the last Nightlight.

5. No Nightlight has ever
slept. They cannot.
They are always awake
to fight nightmares.

6. A Nightlight must
never kiss or be kissed
by a mortal.

7. No one knows what will
happen if that happens.

8. Except that I know I was
kissed by Nightlight.

9. And soon after,
Nightlight slept.

10. And now everyone
is worried.

CHAPTER FIFTEEN

The Pause that Thickens (the Plot, that Is)

EVERY GUARDIAN, EACH IN their separate realm, was hearing every word Katherine read. The Man in the Moon was remembering the events, for he had seen them firsthand. North, Bunnymund, Toothiana, and Sandy were hearing this story in such detail for the first time.

Pitch, however, knew a very different side of this story. From inside his prison, he listened intently to every detail Katherine read. *He* had been there for the creation of this last of the Nightlights. *He* had been the closest friend and protector of the Lunanoff royal family. *He* had been godfather to the baby prince. But he had made a mistake. He did not know the power of the kiss. And *that* had led to his ruin. So now he listened. He listened like he'd never listened to anything before. He was certain that this time he would hear the one twist in the tale that would tell him what he needed most to know.

From the Journal of Katherine While on the Moon

Our time on the Moon has been a mad mix of amazements, beauty, and commotion. The Moon itself is serene past description. Its gray-white surface

is soft and rimmed with stones worn
smooth from centuries of spiraling
through space.

Since coming into orbit with our
Earth, the native Moon creatures have
groomed the outer terrain into sculpted
mountains and valleys of whimsical
and graceful shapes. The same has
been done to the ancient craters that
are scattered near and far. Alas, even
the strongest telescope on Earth isn't
yet powerful enough to bring these
cheerful details into focus, but as I
have traveled with Nightlight to every
harbor of this enchanting place, I've
seen up close the marvels that dot
its every view and crevice. As quiet
as the surface is, its interior has the

hurdy-gurdy dazzlement of a world's
fair—a series of hollowed-out chambers
and halls connected by dozens of
tunnels. These chambers function as
lodgings, dormitories, suites, studies,
laboratories, libraries, banquet halls,
ballrooms, storage places, engine
rooms, and repairing bays, and every
inch is in a constant state of hubbub.
There are even huge pools for sublunar
swimming and underground lakes large
enough to sail upon.

Nightlight borrowed a small Moon
schooner and sailed us across one
such lake. I can say with certainty
that whatever enchantments there may
be throughout the universe, there are
few as stirring and beautiful as sailing

between the spiraling stalagmites of
a subterranean lunar lake illuminated
by glowing shafts of starlight. The
source of our breeze was of equal
enchantment. The whistling rocks
were large and numerous, and did, in
fact, whistle. Their tunes brought a
gentle wind that filled our sail.

Nightlight steered this small but
elegant yacht with quiet assurance. I
had no notion that he could captain a
ship, but his expertise was no surprise.
In truth, he seemed to be good at
every task presented him. I wondered,
not for the first time, how many
talents he must possess.

But he was changing, in swift but
subtle ways. His suit, which had

always glistened with what seemed an inner light, was dimming. The many moonstones that had adorned it for all the time I had known him were falling steadily away. I was not sure if he ignored their loss or simply did not notice, but I know they must be important. The Man in the Moon had given me a special pouch to keep the stones in. I gathered every gem that fell.

"Nightlight will change," MiM told me then. "As will you. But you will become the keeper of his past."

The Man in the Moon told me of so many changes that were perhaps in store for Nightlight and myself. I would grow up, that much was certain. But who or what Nightlight would

become even MiM did not know. I
preferred to focus on our time on that
most improbable lake, a lake that
seemed more dreamed than real, and
I banished all thoughts outside the
wistful perfection of the breeze that
sent us forward.

Nightlight was never very talkative,
but I always understood what he was
feeling. His manner of speaking was
so simple and childlike. He called
danger "the run-or-fight." Grown-ups
were "the Tall Ones" and children
were "the Small Ones," and he always
called me "my Katherine."
    That has changed. He speaks
now in a more mature, almost-adult

Katherine and Nightlight

manner. We sail often on the lunar
lake. It is where Nightlight seems
happiest and most at ease. He tells
me of the dream he had on our way
to the Moon. This seems to have had
a profound effect on him. It was his
first dream, and he is astonished by
the notion of dreaming—that he could
experience something that feels so
real but is not. In his Moondream he
is not a Nightlight but a human boy,
and he lives with a family. There's a
boy and a younger sister and a pair of
kind and caring parents. He speaks
of feeling that he belongs and is cared
for and that he can be wild and free
like any human child. He talks of
these things as though they were exotic

and amazing. He has never known that kind of life. He has always been a Nightlight, and Nightlights do the caring and protecting.

It is poignant to listen to him describe this Moondream. I have never understood how outside of the comforting rhythms of life he has always lived. He longs for the life of, as he calls it, "a regular boy."

There are most unwelcome reports from the outposts at the edge of the Moon's darkscape. Moonbot scouts have observed Pitch himself building a massive army of Nightmare Men. We are trying desperately to contact the other Guardians on Earth, but the entire planet is enshrouded in a storm of dark clouds and no communication can be made, not even with our mind-meld powers. Has Pitch's daughter, Mother Nature, taken his side? Does she make sure the other Guardians cannot help us?

I am so impressed with the Moon's eccentric citizens. Their preparations for the coming battle with Pitch are inspiring. Sweet souls these creatures are, but they are also dogged, well-trained warriors. Under the Man in the Moon's direction, they have set all their defenses around a mountain range called the Ten Bluffs. These ten mountains form a circle that surrounds a taller peak that rises in the center. Between the outer peaks is a shorter series of cliffs and escarpments that make a natural connecting wall. This wall gives the Ten Bluffs the appearance of an otherworldly castle, and the armies of the Moon know every path and crevice, every natural defensive position the rocky fortress offers.

Along these mountainous walls the Moonbot armies stand ready. Their metal chest plates are shined and polished, and every Bot carries a light spear and a crystal sword. The Moonmice have special hideouts farther down the bluffs from which to spy upon any enemy that may

approach. They carry small but potent
light cannons and bombs.

Light is the enemy of Pitch and
his dark armies, so the weapons
used against him have an element of
concentrated phosphorescence: either
from stars, our sun, comets, meteors,
or the illuminates of the glowworms.

The Moon's glowworms are gigantic.
Each is roughly the size of a train
car. Despite their size, they are gentle
creatures with a helpful disposition.
Across their backs and stomachs
run pairs of evenly spaced, brightly
glowing pendants that are used to
help illuminate the many tunnels and
valleys of the Moon. The tips of their
substantial antennae are equipped with

orbs that can dim and brighten at will.
These tips can also shoot concentrated
bombs of light during battle, and at
bedtime they make for a lovely way to
read.

In addition, the glowworms can
hum. Beautifully. Any tune. Eventually,
glowworms evolve into the even more
formidable Lunar Moths, which serve

Glowworms

these furry behemoths can carry a full
cargo of comet rockets attached to
their stomachs and as many as eight
Moonbot Illumineers on their backs.

The Moonbot Illumineers are the
core of the Moon defenders. They're
tough, nearly unstoppable robots.

Lunar Moths

continue their selfless, valiant service
to the Man in the Moon, and they
are now also the keepers of good
dreams. Inside each Illumineer there
lives a precious dream of a human
child. These dreams are the internal
power that sustains the Moonbots,
but they are also the precious cargo
that the Bots protect from all harm. A
Moonbot may become too damaged
or torn to move or fight, but inside
its unbreakable chest plate, the child-
dream will remain forever safe.
These dreams are the long and short
of why the Man in the Moon exists.

A troop of Moonbot Illumineers

In these few fraught days I've come
to understand a simple truth about the
Moon and its king. All his armies and
works are in pursuit of a single goal:
to keep the dreams of children safe.
Their hopes, their cheerful imaginings,
no matter how silly or impossible,
are protected and kept forever. To the
Man in the Moon and his helpers,
these dreams are the brightest light
in all the universe and therefore the
greatest force there is.

The Earth is still covered in clouds,
but we have received distressing
reports. The Man in the Moon sends
thousands of moonbeams down to
Earth every night. Their job is to

search for any signs of Earthly trouble and to chase away small bands of Nightmares. Since the storm began, none of the moonbeams had been able to make it back to the Moon, but tonight several dozen managed to break through the clouds.

They tell us the alarming news that the four of the five great relics of the Golden Age had been stolen from the separate strongholds of the Guardians during the night of celebration after winning the War of Dreams. Nightmare Men had taken each relic. But for what purpose? These relics are the supreme source of power for the Guardians. North's magic sword, Bunnymund's all-powerful egg, Toothiana's ruby box, and the Sandman's Dreamsand.

The Man in the Moon is deeply troubled. He is certain that Pitch himself engineered the stealing of the relics and now plans to take the fifth and last relic. If Pitch finds this last relic, MiM fears that he will be able to vanquish the Guardians, and the Moon itself will be doomed. MiM's expression grew most severe and worried. He takes us to the remnants of his parents' old quarters to the once-beautiful section of the Moon's golden structures. They are scorched and melted, but we can still see their shattered grandeur. Then he tells us that Nightlight is the fifth relic, the

last and most powerful relic of the
Golden Age. "Within each Nightlight
is the energy of a star," MiM
explained. "No other creature in the
universe has more power.

"Pitch will attack from the Moon's
shadow side," he continued. "And he
will come for Nightlight." He says
this with a certainty that cannot be
dismissed.

I'm terrified for my Nightlight,
but he is calm, stoic even. Then
Nightlight seemed to become
somehow older, or less like a boy.
"I think I always knew this deep
inside my heart," he says quietly. "It
frightened me to think I had such
strength.

"I know what I must do," he tells
us. "I must dream."

The Man in the Moon nods. He
seems to understand that this may be
the key to our survival.

MiM escorts us to his childhood
bedroom. Nightlight lays upon the
beautiful, ornate bed. MiM takes a
handful of his own Dreamsand, saved
from when, long ago, Nightlight
had guarded *him*, and he smooths it
across Nightlight's brow. The sand
works quickly. Nightlight smiles at me
as he falls asleep. He lays there, still
as death, but I can feel that something
extraordinary is happening inside
him. Waves of light radiate from him,

filling the room and reflecting off the high, domed ceiling. Moonbots stand guard by the door to stop any attempt by Pitch to attack or abduct him. I stand next to his bed. Each wave of light gives me hope. I touch his forehead. My hand seems to glow. I stroke his unruly white hair. There is no taming it.

Meanwhile, there is a secret mission taking place on the Moon's Dark Side. The hope is to find Pitch's headquarters and discover his plan of attack. Nightlight's original moonbeam, which had lived in his staff through many a battle, will lead the mission along with six Moonmice

inside a tiny flying machine, the Dark
Side Obtruder. I want desperately
to help, but the Man in the Moon
has forbidden me to do so. It is too
dangerous, he says.

"Besides," he tells me, "your—
courage is large, but the ship is small."

I hate that he is correct.

The Moonmice and a moonbeam
came to me after dinner. (A delicious
green cheese omelet. Apparently, a
herd of several cows from the Milky
Way jumped over the Moon, and
several landed here. Now these Moon
cows supply much of the Moon's
fabled green cheese.) The lead
Moonmouse, First Officer Muffet,

described to me an interesting plan
that, if implemented, would make my
joining their mission possible (despite
the Man in the Moon's concerns).
Evidently, they have at their disposal
a sort of shrink ray that can be used
to reduce my size to that of a mouse!
I am instantly hopeful—I'd be able
to fit in the Dark Side Obtruder.
They insist that I go on this mission
because:

1. They like me.

2. They think I'm smart.

3. They think I'm brave.

4. They like me.

5. What the Man in the
   Moon doesn't know won't
   hurt him.

How can I argue?
I am to be shrunk at bedtime, and
we leave at midnight. Fingers of every
size are crossed.

The shrink ray worked splendidly! I
am exactly 2.75 inches tall. Luckily,
the ray shrank my clothes as well. The
moonbeam and the mice hid me in
the back of the Dark Side Obtruder,
so when the Man in the Moon bid the
ship and crew good luck, I remained
undetected.

The obtruder is an ingenious little
vessel—compact, swift, stealthy, and

about the size of an adult's shoe. I sat just behind the moonbeam while he steered, and the Moonmice sat in pairs behind us, reading maps, making calculations, and doing other spyish busywork. We traveled at several hundred feet above the lunar surface until we reached the edge of the Dark Side, then we descended quickly to just a few feet over the shadowy ground. There, we stayed above the surface, rising and swaying among the irregular rocks and craters. This side of the Moon is always in dark twilight, and there is an unmistakably haunted quality to the landscape.

All the tunnels to the Dark Side were sealed long ago for no other

reason than the region felt so mournful
and bleak. These uneasy feelings gave
way to an urgent reality, as we saw
plentiful evidence to confirm that
Pitch is planning a lunar Armageddon.
There are curious trails twined along
the powdery ground. The moonbeam
dimmed himself to just an ember,
and all lights within the obtruder were
turned off. The moonbeam and I
looked out the front windows while the
Moonmice watched from the portholes
as quietly as, well, mice. In the meager
light the only thing that we could see
clearly were the multitudes of stars
above, and they gave us some comfort.
Yes, even in this eerie place, the sight
of stars have that power.

As we wondered where these trails could lead to, a cluster of stars suddenly went dark. Something was blocking the sky! A giant blackness was moving toward us. We could not make out what this Thing was. It was as dark as the sky, and the only hint we had of its size and shape was from the shifting absence of the stars that it blackened.

The moonbeam brought the obtruder to a halt. As we hovered behind a column of rocks, we could begin to make sense of this wandering blackness. It was gigantic, an irregularly shaped oval, and extending from this oval, we saw a goodly number of spiderlike legs that must have been three hundred feet in height. The Thing moved gracefully and in almost complete silence. It was walking slightly to the right of us. We assumed it had not seen us, for it continued past. We followed carefully. We were keeping pace with it when we began to hear a low rumbling from behind. Before we could turn, a vast wave of galloping shapes rolled just beneath us, a steady tide of blackness much darker than the Moonscape.

"A herd of horses!" I whispered, astonished.

"Miss Katherine is correct," said First Officer Muffet.

"A herd of actual Nightmares," said Ensign Tuffet, another ranking

The Dark Side Crawler aka the Nightmare Cyclops Spider

Moonmouse on our mission.

Nightmares indeed! And each one ridden by a Nightmare Man. I looked at the moonbeam in alarm. Communication with the Man in the Moon or anyone on the Bright Side of the Moon is impossible from the Dark Side, so we had to sneak away as soon as possible and sound the alarm.

"How can we find out more?" I asked the moonbeam.

The moonbeam nodded to the Moonmice, then piloted the obtruder closer to the main body of the giant spider craft. It was picking its way at a steady pace toward the border of the Moon's Bright Side.

Once we were within a dozen feet

of the spider, we saw the craft was literally coated with thousands of Nightmare Men and other creatures of the night, churning and swaying as the spider glided along. We edged even closer, our small size and the darkness keeping us from being detected. There appeared to be a round window at the front of the body of the spider craft. In the window's glow we saw the silhouette of a figure. This gave the craft the appearance of having a single large eye. Then I realized that the figure at the center of this evil eye was Pitch himself!

"Only Pitch could conceive of a thing so fearsome," murmured Ensign Tuffet.

"A Nightmare Cyclops Spider,"
First Officer Muffet added with a
shudder.

I was frightened too. Still, I urged
the moonbeam to go closer. "We
must see if he has the four relics," I
explained.

The moonbeam, ever brave,
inched us to the outside edge of the
window. As we hovered, he rotated
the obtruder so that we were better
able to see inside. In the center of the
dark oval room was a large, strangely
shaped container riveted to the floor
with a series of hulking bolts. The
material it was made of—at least
its outside—I recognized! I pressed
against the window of our obtruder

for a better look, and then I was certain. The container was molded from the Nightmare Rock that I had been imprisoned within when Pitch had tried to make me his Darkling Daughter. I pulled away from the window, a chill running through me.

What was Pitch using it for now?

I thought hard. The rock was made of dark matter—the only substance that can block the light that makes him vulnerable. I thought harder. The light Pitch fears most is emitted from the relics! The relics glow with Golden Age light—it is one of the most powerful weapons against him. I pressed against the window once more. The shape of this container was so odd, with lumps and curves and juts of pointed ridges. It looked like a cluster of things, not a single thing.

"Yes, yes! A cluster of things. Of *relics*!" I cried.

"He must cover the relics with dark matter to shield himself from the light they throw," I thought out loud. "But how will he use them against the Man in the Moon and his troops? Golden Age light makes *them* stronger."

"The Man in the Moon will understand what it means," First Officer Muffet suggested.

"We've seen enough," Ensign Tuffet agreed.

The moonbeam shifted into full throttle, and we sped away.

We crossed the border out of the
Dark Side and were now flying toward
the fortress of the Ten Bluffs. First
Officer Muffet and Ensign Tuffet
were trying to radio ahead to MiM, to
anyone, word of what we'd seen.

But there was something amiss.

The mice were shouting (as much
as mice can shout) into their radio
sets. Their comically high voices
sounded urgent, almost angry. They
were talking very fast, repeating
phrases again and again. Their words
were running together like a recording
played at too fast a speed.

"Doyoureadme?Doyoureadme?Ten
Bluffsdoyoureadmeover?!Overover!!"

"Whattheheckistheproblemwhycan't
wegetthrough!!"

"Whywhywhywhywhywhywhy?!"

"BeatsmeIdunnoIdunnoIdunno
Idunno!"

"I'mstressedI'mstressedI'mstressed!"

"MetooMetooMetooMeeeeee
toooooo!"

"What's wrong?" I tried to ask, and
all six mice began answering me at
once while madly flicking at switches
and knobs and levers.

"Wedon'tknowit'sinterference
interferenceinterference!!"

"Pitchit'sPitchit'sPitchmustbePitch
PitchPitchPitch!!!"

I looked at the moonbeam. He was
flickering at full tilt. We all sensed it—

something was in the air. Strangely,
I was not fearful. I could tell that
the moonbeam wasn't either. *Can it
be that I feel Nightlight's presence?*
Then the sky above us brightened with
waves of light, exactly like the ones
in the chamber where Nightlight was
dreaming.

Our engine suddenly went silent.
Everything in the ship stopped working.
We lost all power! Yet the moonbeam
stayed calm and steadily piloted us
closer and closer to the ground. We
were gliding downward at an alarming
speed, just missing rocks and craters.

"Deadmicedeadmicedeadmice
ohwellohwellohwell," the mice were
murmuring.

We were mere feet above the ground now. The moonbeam found a stretch of smooth, sandy surface, and he lowered us carefully upon it. Yikes! A rock! We dodged . . . and missed it by a hairbreath . . . then . . . then . . . with jittery ease, we skimmed along the sands, skipping like a stone on water. We began to slow. It was a harsh and lurching few seconds that felt like forever. Our ship skidded into a half circle as we wobbled and swayed and finally . . . halted, facing backward. We sat still. As if frozen. Were we alive? Yes. The mice began to chatter like windup toys with springs that had sprung.

"Thatwascloseclosecloseso0000o
close!Welivewelivewelivelivelive!"

"Needasnack.Needasnack.
Neeeeeeedaaaaasnnnack!"

"Cheesecheesecheesecheese."

"Curdsandwhey!Curdsandwhey!
Curdsandwhey!"

And indeed they pulled from their
ration boxes cheese, curds, and whey
and began nibbling furiously.

"Would you care for some?" asked
First Officer Muffet, regaining his
normal, less squeaky speaking voice.

"Just the cheese, please," I
responded politely.

The mice began to sigh contentedly,
then returned to their radios as they
munched.

I turned to the moonbeam. "I think those light waves come from Nightlight. I think something remarkable may be happening as he dreams."

The moonbeam flickered in a way that seemed like he agreed with me. I wished Ombric were here. He knew how to translate moonbeam-speak. I wished all the Guardians were here. North. Tooth. Sandy.

"In the battle that is surely coming, we must be braver than we've ever been," I said to the moonbeam.

He dimmed a bit, as if sharing my concern. Then he flashed worriedly. Something was wrong. We again felt a low rumble coming toward us.

Emerging from the Moon's dark
side, we saw Pitch's giant spider craft
coming toward us.

"I think we best make a speedy
getaway," I told the moonbeam.

"Away! Away! Away!" the mice
agreed in unison.

Thankfully, the engine of the
obtruder restarted immediately.
Officers Muffet and Tuffet, along
with the other mice, tossed down
their curds and whey, the moonbeam
piloted us away from Pitch and
his giant mechanical spider, and I
swallowed the last bite of Mooncheese
I may ever eat. Such frightening
goings-on!

We made our way to the Ten Bluffs,
but not without incident. There had
been several more bright flashes in
the sky, and each time our ship had
lost power, forcing us into perilous
landings. The mice had consumed
more dairy than seemed possible or
healthy, but they continued to function
ably so . . . What did I know?

To my great relief, the Ten Bluffs
formed the most formidable fortress
imaginable, with every Moonbot,
mouse, worm, and moth in place,
armed and ready for battle. MiM
had indeed received our messages.
Everyone at the Bluffs knew the nature
of the force that was coming. They
knew Pitch was on his way.

The mice quickly reversed my size
to its original with one zap of the
shrink ray's override button, and I ran
with MiM to check on Nightlight.
But Nightlight still slept.
MiM and I stood on either side of
him. The moonbeam rested on MiM's
shoulder. We were worried for our
beloved friend. What strangeness was
going on inside Nightlight's dream?

We watched for what seemed hours,
then I started to notice that the room
was no longer glowing as it had been.
Had Nightlight's dream ended? I
glanced at MiM, and we both looked
down at Nightlight—he, too, seemed
to have dimmed! The remaining

jewels on his magnificent uniform
had gone dull; they caught less light
than a wax doll. His skin no longer
glimmered with its lovely inner light.
The moonbeam flew and hovered just
above Nightlight's face, but Nightlight
did not stir or wake. His breath
pushed and pulled the moonbeam's
soft glow, but this was the only sign of
life we could see.

MiM caught my eye. "We must let
him continue on his sleep journey.
Let's leave him in peace, shall we?" I
felt too anxious to leave, but at that
very moment—

Bells rang! Horns blared! The
general alarm was sounded! Pitch

and his army must be approaching. I scrambled with MiM out of the room, and we headed to the highest peak of Ten Bluffs. From there, we could see the flat plains of the lunar landscape that surround the Bluffs. There are no other mountains or ridges to give cover to the enemy. But that enemy was vast, inky, and seemingly endless. With it came a deep, unnerving rumble that grew louder and louder, layering us with sound that we could *feel*! Everything was vibrating. It felt like fear itself.

I stared, stunned.

This army of Nightmares was too huge. They were simply too many for us to fight.

I reached for MiM's hand. I'd never
felt so afraid. I battled Pitch many
times, but this felt different, more
sinister. MiM looked me in the eye,
this curious, valiant little man, as round
as the Moon he defends. Dressed not
as a warrior about to face his mortal
enemy, but dandified from head to
foot in the most resplendent suit I had
ever seen. He broke into a perfectly
cheerful, jack-o'-lantern grin. His eyes
were bright, almost merry. I didn't
understand how he could be unafraid.

And then I too felt unafraid.
Suddenly, I believed that there can be a
goodness so pure and bright and strong
that no darkness could ever extinguish
it. MiM nodded. He knew what I was

thinking. Then he spun around to face
Pitch's army. He put his spyglass to his
eye with a confident snap. He swung
the scope to the right, to the left, then,
without looking away from his glass,
he told the Moonbot Illumineer beside
him, "Let loose the Lunars."

Commands were shouted. The
Moonbot troops began to toot
their war horns, and the sky filled
with Lunar Moths diving toward the
dark hordes that were beginning to
surround us. The moths strafed and
bombed the enemy, diving in low to
make sure they hit their mark. Light
bombs detonated as bright as meteors.
With each explosion, a dazzling spot
appeared on the lunar landscape as

Nightmare Men were wiped clean, but their replacements refilled the void far too quickly.

And then we saw Pitch's giant Nightmare Cyclops Spider. It was bounding over the rushing mass of Nightmare troops, then took the lead as it clambered at the edges of Ten Bluffs. Its many legs scrambled at a freakish speed and stabbed at the ground with a savagery terrible to behold. The Moonmice would soon be under its treading.

"He means to overwhelm us by sheer numbers," MiM observed, handing me a second spyglass from his waistcoat.

And indeed this seemed likely.

There were so very, very many of every variety of Pitch's wicked troops. With our spyglasses, we could see Pitch clearly. He sat at what appeared to be the controls of a large, oddly shaped, cannonlike gun.

"That's it! The four relics combined," I told MiM, for I was sure it was the thing I had glimpsed when we were on our mission. MiM was impressed by my observation, though he was less than pleased that I had disobeyed his orders to stay behind. He frowned at me in the way a loving grandfather would. And then his expression softened. I felt he was more proud of my accomplishment than he was angry at my disobedience.

"So it seemed Pitch has covered himself in a cloak of dark matter; that's how he can use the light of the relics against us. The combined light of all the relics was too powerful even for the Guardians. The cloak will protect him," muttered the Man in the Moon. Then his smile grew beatific. "He will not succeed." The mice were clustered in rocky bivouacs along the slopes.

"Tell the mice to fire," MiM ordered.

No sooner did he say this than thousands of moon missiles streaked through the skies and decimated the first wave of Nightmare cavalry. Then the second wave. And the third.

But Pitch charged on, acting as a
protective screen for all his troops
behind him, forming a sort of gigantic
spear of Nightmare soldiers, with
the spider craft as the deadly tip.
With startling swiftness, the spider
scaled its way up the steep rise of
the outer peaks and to the rim of the
mountainous wall. The Moonbots
sent a hail of fire from every angle,
and the spider paused, but only so
the Nightmare soldiers it carried
could leap down upon the Bots. They
battled hand to hand.

The fortress of the Ten Bluffs
was now like an island completely
surrounded by a moat of Nightmare
Men. Hundreds of Lunar Moths

dove and raked the dark monsters
that pressed relentlessly toward us.
Thousands of light bullets and bombs
shot out at the waves of Nightmare
troops, turning the night into a
terrible, constant pulsing of blinding
light and flames.

Then an awful sort of hum cut
through the chaos of sounds. It must
have been the relic weapon powering
up. Pitch was aiming it at us!

"Engage the mirror shields," MiM
commanded sharply.

Giant, round, mirrorlike devices
emerged from the ground and angled
themselves toward Pitch's vessel.
A beam of scorching bright light
blistered out from Pitch's weapon—he

had fired! But his aim was faulty;
the beam hit the rocks below us.
The force of it, however, pulverized a
hunk of the fortress, sending a deluge
of rocks and boulders down upon
the battlements below. I feared that
another hit of that strength would
cause our whole bluff to collapse.

But MiM remained calm.

A second blast erupted. This time
it was blocked by the mirrors and
was instantly deflected. It angled back
toward Pitch.

He'll be destroyed for sure, I
thought, but I was wrong.

The beam engulfed the spider craft
and shattered the rock wall beneath
it. But with one awful jump, the

machine escaped the light and landed halfway up our bluff. MiM and I ran to the edge of the bluff wall. Smoke poured from Pitch's ship as it clawed and stabbed its way up to us. The top portion was scorched and peeled away. Pitch, too, was scorched and smoldering, charred almost black, but the whites of his eyes shimmered. He was still secure beneath his protective cloak. We could see him smiling as his hideous machine quickly closed the distance between us.

On every side of Ten Bluffs the battle thundered. The clash of Nightmare and Moon troops was intense beyond measure. How any creature of darkness or light could survive, I could not imagine, but the Moon defenses held in all but one small breach—where Pitch and his vessel scaled the outer wall. It was like a hole in a dam, but enough of a hole to allow Nightmares to stream into the fortress. They were a force that could not be contained.

The Bots were shoulder to shoulder, firing their light rifles in unison. Each volley vaporized the leading line of the Nightmares but stopped their advance only for a moment. They managed to creep a few precious feet closer. With lightning speed, the Bots formed into more rows. The front row kneeled and fired. Within an instant, the row behind them

fired. Row after row, firing, firing.
The Nightmares still advanced, but
now only by inches. Pitch could not
tolerate this pace. He gunned his
motor. Ten thousand light bullets
rained down upon him. The spider
craft was being chipped away, but it
still held. And Pitch's dark matter
shield withstood the onslaught.

Then Pitch was upon us. He made
it over the bluff edge. MiM pulled
me behind him. The spider's legs
pierced and stabbed at the valiant
Moonbots, tossing them away like
toys. Moonbots quickly turned the
half dozen reflectors to protect us,
but the spider's front legs jabbed and
shattered the reflector mirrors. Pitch

halted his vehicle a dozen feet from us, aiming the relic weapon directly at us.

"You'll go no farther, Pitch!" shouted MiM above the din of the battle. "You'll never get the boy!"

MiM raised his lunar staff as the spider's legs lunged at us, but MiM was more than up to the task. The little round man deftly deflected each jab with his staff, then broke off the spider's front two legs with one neat sweep. Pitch was surprised. He paused his attack.

"It is no boy I seek, but a Nightlight!" he bellowed down at us. "The *only* Nightlight. He is the last relic! And with his heart, I will finally rid my own soul of the last glimmer of

light that lives within me. I will finally
be rid of any feeling other than hate.
Hate for all things good."

MiM stood his ground. "One more
step, and by all the powers of my
parents and the stars above, you will
be destroyed!"

"I fear no star," Pitch roared back.
"I fear no power! And I don't fear *you*!

"THEN FEAR *ME*," came a
laughing voice from behind us. A
voice both familiar, yet not.

It was Nightlight!

With the speed of a hawk,
Nightlight dove and landed on one
knee between the spider and us. I
could not see him well—the light that
glowed from the relic cannon was

nearly blinding. Then he slowly stood
to face Pitch. His uniform was gone.
He was dressed plainly in only a blue
hooded shirt and brown leggings, and
no shoes at all. His white hair was still
wild but shorter. With his clenched
fists on either hip, his stance was
almost insultingly calm and defiant.

Nightlight looked over his shoulder
to MiM and me and smiled. It was
a smile like no other. It was not the
childlike smile of the Nightlight I
have known. There was something
a bit wild and prankish in it. But it
was a good smile. A jovial smile. A
"follow me" smile.

He turned back to Pitch and
pointed to the relic weapon. "You

shouldn't steal other peoples' toys, Pitch. Especially if you don't know how to play with them!"

Then he pulled his diamond dagger from his shirt and seemed ready to spring at Pitch. The blade glowed bright. And I saw the moonbeam! Nightlight's moonbeam was in the blade and was ready to guide the sharp tip to Pitch's black heart.

Pitch laid his damaged hand over his heart as if to protect it—the hand that still held the locket with the picture of his daughter. "You'll never bring light to my heart again, little man. I'll burn you like coal and use your blackened bones to make my evil complete!"

Then Pitch aimed the weapon
directly at Nightlight. But something
stopped him. He looked past
Nightlight, and seemingly past us.
MiM and I turned as well. Everything
around us seemed to be moving
in slow motion. Then we saw a
most welcome sight. Arriving on a
fleet of hastily constructed airships
were Ombric, North, Bunnymund,
Toothiana, and Sandman, and pouring
down from the sky were all the
armies they command.
Legions of tooth
fairies, elves,
Yetis, and
Warrior
Eggs of

every size. My heart surged. Even old
friends like Petrov, North's valiant
horse, and the great bear of Santoff
Claussen had come! They had
somehow broken away from stormy
Earth and made their way to us. They
joined the Moonbot troops and,
within moments, were overwhelming
the Nightmare hordes.

And still every movement was
unnaturally slowed down. I saw
Ombric leading the way, and it
dawned on me: The great wizard was
slowing time.

Pitch triggered his weapon. Its
blinding light emerged in slow
motion, like a column of glowing
clay. Using all of his powers, Ombric

waded through this slowing of time
to block the ray from consuming
Nightlight. Raising his arms above his
head, he fanned out his cloak until it
made a near-perfect circle that shielded
us all from the death beam that crept
closer. From that moment, we who
were behind Ombric regained our
normal sense of time while everything
in front of him grew slower still.
North and the other Guardians stood
with us.

Nightlight looked to the open sky,
his diamond dagger held aloft with its
moonbeam glowing. And in a fraction
of a second he vanished, vanished into
the heavens. I stared after him. Where
was he going? Why?

Pitch stared as well, and his fury
became unhinged. The old wizard was
struggling against the intensity of the
relic weapon's ray as Pitch fired again
and again. North waved for us to join
him in readying one of the reflectors
so as to give Ombric aid. But I could
not keep from worrying about the full
meaning of Nightlight's leaving.

The reflector jammed; it was stuck
and would not move. North and Sandy
were pushing at it with all of their might,
but Ombric seemed to be disintegrating
in the savage brilliance of the ray. Then
an even brighter light filled the entire
sky. It was a dazzling, unnatural light,
brighter than a dozen suns. All fighting
ceased. No being, good or evil, could

help but be mesmerized at the sight of a light so confounding.

I could hear Pitch's coarse breathing in the sudden quiet. He sounded . . . afraid. Afraid of what was coming.

As we all looked skyward, the light splintered into seven separate points, like stars, but more radiant than any star I've ever seen.

"It is the Seven Stars of the Nightlights," said MiM in awe.

And as he said this, the seven stars arranged themselves into what appeared to be a giant constellation of a single face. From it came a voice so deep and full that I could feel it as much as hear it.

"Our brother Nightlight will not be yours, Pitch," the voice boomed.

"Your schemes are finished, and we
are finished with you!"

Then from the constellation came
a great enveloping of their light.
It wrapped around the Nightmare
Armies, melting and molding them
into giant clots that began to encircle
Pitch. These clots condensed and
calcified until they became super
concentrated darkness. They became
dark matter. A single lashlike strand
of the light knotted around the relic
weapon and snapped it away from
Pitch's clutches, instantly separating it
into its four distinct pieces. The egg
on its staff, the sword, the Dreamsand,
and the ruby box. The relics spiraled
into the waiting hands of their true

owners, Bunnymund, North, Sandy, and Tooth. In the unsettled air their capes and coats billowed. We were all thinking the same thing: *We are the Guardians of Childhood, and we will fight to the last if need be.*

But we did not need to. The waves of light continued to turn the Nightmare Army into a mass of molten darkness that engulfed Pitch until only his face and chest were left exposed. He seemed to be struggling to free one hand.

With one tremendous thrust, his arm broke through the thickening mass that was imprisoning him. Then we saw his hand. It still held the locket with the small cameo of his daughter. It had been

melted, fused to his palm and fingers.
Wild with panic, Pitch looked to North.
He pounded his chest. "Please! I have
failed every being I have ever held dear!
Use your sword! I cannot bear this
goodness that still lives in my heart."

It is hard to have sympathy for a
creature that has tried to destroy you,
but in that moment I did. I felt sorry
for the pitiful thing Pitch had become.

We all felt pity for Pitch in that
awful moment. But the Seven
Stars of the Nightlights did not.
They had seen the ways of evil. They
knew its many tricks. Good hearts
will always have sympathy, but the
wisdom of stars is clear and powerful
and more true. They knew that death

was not the answer for Pitch.

The melted essence of Pitch's Nightmare Army spun round and round the Nightmare King. His hand that held the ruined picture of Emily Jane was now pinned against his chest at the spot just over his heart. "*Pleeeeease,*" he moaned to North, to all of us. "*Pleeeease* let me die."

North could take no more. If there was any hate in North's great heart, it was for Pitch. But to be imprisoned with the heartache, pain, and sorrow that Pitch faced seemed a misery worse than *any* creature should bear.

So North gripped his relic sword and marshaled every power it possessed. He lunged forward, his

sword's tip bright with the ancient
power of the Golden Age. There was
no force known that could stop it.

And yet . . .

As the sword's tip pierced the
weathered paper of Pitch's daughter's
portrait, then sliced through Pitch's hand,
and then bore down farther, entering the
flesh over the Nightmare King's heart, a
strobe of light flashed. A hand grasped
the sword and stopped it cold.

It was Nightlight!

He stared at North, holding the
blade so hard, his own hand bled. "You
must not stain your soul or end the one
chance Pitch has to save his own from
darkness."

With that, he moved the sword away

from Pitch's chest. As
he did, we saw a small
trickle of black blood
ooze from the paper of
Emily Jane's cameo. It
was Pitch's blood, and it was
mixing with Nightlight's. The two
began to spread across the paper, but in
a miraculous way. The blood made the
image of Emily Jane bright again.

Barely able to move his head, Pitch
strained and strained until he could see
the cameo pressed against his heart . . .
see the face of his beloved daughter return.

Nightlight backed away, and we all
watched as the dark matter began to
twine over Pitch's chest and face. We
watched as our enemy wept silently,

Emily Jane, Pitch's daughter

tears as clear as crystals. No one had thought the Nightmare King was capable of tears, but Nightlight knew otherwise. He reverently dabbed them into his wounded hand and clutched them tightly. Within a moment, a new diamond dagger had materialized. Nightlight tucked it into his shirt before any of us could glimpse it.

Nightlight turned and reached for MiM's hand and mine, then addressed us all with urgency.

"I must go now. I must go see if the rest of my Moondream will play out." He pressed my hand more tightly. "I have a journey to take, and I don't know when we will see each other again." He spoke quickly and surely,

but his voice cracked as he continued.
"But know this: You will see me
again. You must trust that and believe
it." His eyes implored us.

"I do," I said. The others nodded.

The waves of molten matter
finished winding around Pitch. He
was completely overwhelmed and
entombed, like an Egyptian king in a
sarcophogus from which he could not
escape. What was left was a cooling,
lumpy sphere that resembled a small
black moon. With one graceful leap,
Nightlight was atop the sphere. He
looked at us. Each of us. He was so
changed. He seemed almost like a
human boy now. Then he looked up
at the Nightlight constellation and

nodded, as if to show he was ready.
The many waves of light spiraled and
circled above us and began to braid
together like a giant rope, then dove
toward the black sphere, hitting it with
such force that it rocketed away into
space. It was streaking toward
Earth like a comet, with
Nightlight straddling
atop, seeming to
guide it.

Katherine paused her reading. What caused her to pause was the memory of that last moment with Nightlight. She would not see him again for more than a hundred years.

"Shall I continue?" she asked Jack.

Jack was now crouched close by the fire. Yet Katherine noticed that a pattern of frost radiated out from where he sat. The room had grown so chilly that she could see her breath, and she recognized yet another change in her friend—whenever he was deep in concentration or felt danger, he often brought a chill to the air.

In one hand he held Twiner, the staff leaning close to his right ear. His other hand rested on his knee, with his thumb and forefinger extended upward as if pointing. A thin stream of smoke from the fire looped and spiraled to the tip of his finger while another rope of smoke came out of this thumb and twirled up to his left ear. The smoke proceeded out of his right ear and into Twiner.

Katherine had forgotten that Jack could talk to

firewood. That through their smoke, he could listen to the wood's history and stories. Sometimes he received messages from forests in this way. All trees remained connected, even after being cut or even burned. Their ash and smoke were absorbed by their still-living brethren.

Now she felt a flash of irritation. Had Jack even been listening to what she'd been reading?

"I am listening to you, Katherine," he said, reading her mind.

"I'm sure," she replied tartly. "I hope the firewood has equally interesting stories to tell."

"Not quite," he said, "but still rather compelling."

"Did you remember what you needed?" she asked.

"It helped a great deal," he replied. "But . . . now I need to do the telling. There are things you don't know, that aren't in Mr. Qwerty's pages. We must hurry, though. There isn't much time."

His tone told her that he had heard something important from the firewood.

"Are we in danger?" she asked. "The Raconturks are on guard. They are very—"

"We are fine," he interrupted. "For now."

Jack so seldom lied to her. But Katherine felt certain that danger must be close at hand. He was choosing to take a calculated risk and continue to tell her what he needed to. So the telling must be very important.

Indeed it was. Jack needed to tell her about those years he was gone. He needed to fill in the missing pages of his journey. He needed to tell her how he had taken the name Jack Frost . . . and why.

And so he began the story of Jack Frost.

THE TESTIMONY OF
JACKSON OVERLAND FROST
AS TRANSCRIBED BY THE BOOK
KNOWN AS MR. QWERTY
TO KATHERINE OF GANDERLY,
DECEMBER 27, 1933

The power of a Nightlight is formidable, especially just before he is released from his oath, the oath to protect a royal child of the Golden Age. Once I had fulfilled that oath to MiM, I should have become a star and joined my fellow Nightlights as a hopeful but distant constellation. In that moment of transforming, the power inside me would have become strong enough to burn the last bit of goodness that lived inside Pitch's black heart.

Pitch knew this.

He intended to capture me and focus that power through the ray of the relic weapon. He planned to aim the ray at his own heart and rid himself of his last weakness. I would likely have been destroyed, along with everyone on the Moon, and quite likely on Earth as well.

But I had already found *you*, Katherine. And with our kiss, I had taken a new oath. Not in words, but in my heart.

This had never happened to a Nightlight. A Nightlight cannot have two oaths. And so I began to change, to become not a star, but something new.

Unwittingly, I had thwarted Pitch's plan.

No other Nightlight has ever had the life I've had. The others have stayed with their child till that child was grown up. There is a moment when a child passes over to that different place—the place of grown-ups. From the time children are very small, they want to do what grown-ups do, the million small amazements that grown-ups seem masters of: to know how things work; how to get to places and somehow know the way back; how to read and write; how to button buttons and tie shoes; knowing when food is ready; and being able to reach the top shelf. They want to do this all.

Finally, facts and knowledge outweigh the daydreams and fancies, and it is the Nightlight's job to protect the wonder as his child wanders into this land of grown-ups.

But I did not stay with my prince. By saving him from Pitch at the last battle of the Golden Age, I was forced to leave him. I could only hope that he had made his way with his sense of wonder still intact. So it was an enormous relief when we were finally face-to-face after our journey back to the Moon. I knew for certain that my prince had grown up grand. Grand in spirit and wisdom. And so I should have joined my brother Nightlights.

I knew our kiss had changed that fate.

I was no longer a true Nightlight. What was I to become?

To have no clue about one's fate is a strange and fearful feeling. I had no place in any story I could see: I could not be of the Golden Age, and yet I could not be human. Inside, I knew I was both, and neither. But then my Moondream showed me another path.

My Moondream was long and epic. In the first part I flew up to the stars of my brother

Nightlights and told them of our kiss. They told me I must follow my Moondream and shine not as a star, but as a boy on Earth. And they swore to help me. And so they did. The battle played out as I'd dreamed it. As did my guiding Pitch's dark meteor to Santoff Claussen. There, my old friends—Petter, Sascha, Tall William, William the Almost Youngest, William the Absolute Youngest, the owls, the squirrels, the Spirit of the Forest, even the mechanical djinni—were at the ready to help if necessary.

Also waiting to help was one more—one who was not from Santoff Claussen. Emily Jane, Pitch's daughter, Mother Nature herself, drew upon her great store of atmospheric energy and fury to help fashion her father's prison under Big Root. She had already tricked her father into believing that she had caused the Earth-covering storm to cut off communication from the Moon to the Guardians in these desperate days before the Battle of Bright Night, but all the while she was secretly helping them plan their rescue mission.

Emily Jane could sense that her father's blood now coursed through my veins, sense that she and I were now bound together, almost like a brother and sister. It was in this strange way that I finally had a family. That I belonged, by blood, to others.

The Guardians had left instructions with the villagers before the Battle of Bright Night: Should they not return from the Moon, Emily Jane would be in charge of keeping Santoff Claussen safe.

With the ground near Big Root still aglow from the impact of Pitch's meteor, Emily Jane gathered every citizen and creature together. She laid out all her needs and plans, her resolution bringing a quiet determination to all.

"For many years Santoff Claussen has been designed to keep Pitch out," she explained. "Now we must work to keep him in. It must be remembered that the man you call Pitch was once a great hero. He tried to halt the spread of darkness, but the darkness was too strong, and despite his desperate fight, it overtook him. Now it will be our job to keep that darkness contained. Santoff Claussen will become a prison, for Pitch and for the dark that lives inside him. Only a place of great courage and light can fight this darkness. That place is here, and its warriors are you."

The response was unequivocal. To the last man, woman, child, squirrel, and leaf, Santoff Claussen would do whatever needed doing to keep Pitch contained.

But *I* knew Emily Jane was secretly hoping for more. She was hoping that, somehow, her father would find redemption. That he would win his battle over the darkness that had curdled his once-noble heart.

She wanted her father back. She wanted the one loving thing that was left of her childhood to return. Only through a miracle could this happen. But even before I was part human, I knew that believing in miracles was the beating heart inside every mortal. It's what keeps them going no matter how dreadful the odds.

As I left for the last part of my Moondream, the skies around us rumbled. Weather is often at the mercy of Emily Jane's moods. Though her voice was calm, the skies said otherwise as she told me, "My heart fears for you. You spared my father's life, and for that, I am forever in your debt," she added. "You and my father are linked now. How that will evolve, I do not know. Will your goodness affect him? Or will his darkness shadow you?"

The sky cracked with a splinter of lightning, followed by a roll of thunder.

"I will help you however I can. But now you must leave," she said more urgently. "Finish your dream. Disappear if you can. Don't let yourself be found."

Then she placed one hand on the secret pocket where I kept the dagger forged from her father's tears.

"He fears this most. Use it. You'll know how . . . and when."

The look on her face was desperate. The strange

storm, which came from no cloud anyone could see, grew deafening. I opened my cape and let the wind fill it like a sail. Lifting into the sky, I nodded farewell, then left Santoff Claussen in a gale. Rain fell from the cloudless sky. And I realized that the raindrops were from Emily Jane. They were the tears she would not shed.

I knew where I needed to go. The last part of my Moondream had shown me. It was a real place. A farm. Where a boy named Jack lived.

Somehow, I knew the way, and for a while I simply walked in the direction that seemed right. Sometimes I traveled by road, but just as often I walked through open country, sleeping in fields or woods. For the first time in my life, I did entirely as I pleased. But I did not feel lonely in the least. For I had my self, my *new self,* filling my thoughts and feelings. Every moment seemed miraculous: Sunlight, on anything and at any time, was an endless marvel. The golden wash of light that brightens treetops at day's end when the world becomes a twilight of velvet shadows and fading radiance—this became my favorite time of day.

And when night came, I was happy still, for I could feel the light of the stars. I could see my fellow Nightlights and knew they wished me well. They had, after all, given me my Moondream and, with it, my new life. And I could feel MiM watching over me. As yet, I could not talk directly to him or any of the other Guardians; my ability to send thoughts, or read theirs, seemed to be gone. My old powers were at their weakest; I knew not when they might return.

I could feel the other Guardians, too, but only vaguely. They were like the warmth of a story told around a long-ago campfire. I hoped that my weakened powers would at least make it impossible for Pitch to know my whereabouts and for his soldiers to track me.

These days and nights were my school, my playground, my always-unfolding map of who I was becoming. Sometimes I ran with wolves till they became my friends. I traveled with bears and chipmunks, deer and elk, eagles, owls, bats, and moles. If it crawled, flew, dug, or ran, I learned its ways and language. Wild I became, but it was a noble wildness. I never killed unless to eat. I never harmed unless to help. I only fought to make peace. And every night I dreamed new dreams. Such a wonderful, terrifying, joyful world was Dreamland. Oh, I loved to dream.

And all the while I traveled closer toward the boy named Jack.

Then one night I was woken from a dream by a dull pain in my hand, the hand that I'd wounded saving Pitch. A cold wind blew suddenly through the woods where I was camped, and for the first time since my journey began, I felt unease. The wind was surely a warning from Emily Jane. The pain in my hand could only be a sign that Pitch was reaching out in some way. I stayed still and quiet. The Moon was waxing, providing just enough light to give some clarity to the tangle that surrounded me. I heard a curious sound coming nearer and nearer. It was a heavy, constant flattening of fallen leaves and snapping of small sticks, as if something large was moving across the forest floor.

The pain in my hand grew sharper. I knew I was in danger, but from what, I couldn't guess. It was then that I heard a voice!

"It is the Lermontoff Serpent."

I spun around. A man apparently made of sticks stood no more than an arm's length away from me.

"North sent me," the stick man explained. "He made me for you. He wasn't sure if you were still alive, but if you were, he thought I could be useful. My name is Twiner."

"Twiner? How Northian," I remarked. "Is he well?"

The sounds of the serpent sidled closer.

"North is . . . North," said Twiner blandly. "If I may say so, I think you best make use of me before you're swallowed." No sooner did Twiner finish that sentence than he transformed into a wooden

staff with a crooked end that very much reminded me of the staff I had in my Nightlight days, but less ornate. He was, in appearance, just a simple stick.

I heard the crackles and crash of a tree trunk, and I turned to the edge of the small clearing where I camped. There coiled a most imposing creature. Its triangular head alone was larger than I was, its eyes glittered venomously, its long forked tongue flicked with menace.

This was a serpent that was not to be trifled with.

It lunged for me.

I grabbed Twiner.

The fight that followed was full of surprise and interest. Twiner was no simple stick. And I discovered I was no simple human. Together we made a formidable team.

It's interesting how much focus one can achieve when a fifty-foot serpent is trying to devour you. I discovered that my Nightlight powers were not gone but had, how shall I describe it, evolved? Yes, evolved. Sudden moments of invisibility? That was new and convenient. Extraordinary speed? Very handy when a fanged mouth the size of a bathtub is bearing down on you. A wooden staff that could change form from one instant to the next (sword, club, spear, bow)? Most useful and rather fun.

The serpent struck. I dodged. Its long tail cracked like a whip. I vanished. It bit. I blocked it with Twiner in whatever form my instincts thought best.

After a few hectic minutes of battle the serpent was tired, battered, and frustrated while Twiner and I were just finding our stride. The serpent decided to retreat and slithered noisily away. I jammed the slim end of Twiner into the ground so that he stood upright.

"Why was the creature called the Lermontoff Serpent?" I asked.

Twiner became a twig man once again and began to explain.

"He was once an impressive human. An ally, in fact, of Ombric Shalazar. He was the protector of the Valley of Lost Dreams. Pitch, however, turned him into a serpent, and now he hunts the source of Earth's most hopeful dreams."

I gave this some thought.

"You mean he eats people?"

"Yes," Twiner replied. "He eats people who have consistently good dreams."

"Did Pitch send him to eat me?"

"Likely, yes." Twiner sat down. So did I. "You *have* been dreaming rather loudly. You were easy to find," he added.

The adrenaline of battle was fading. I felt extremely tired. My hand no longer ached.

"You should rest," said Twiner. "I'll keep watch."

And so I did sleep. And dreamed. And all was well. Twiner was on watch.

With Twiner as my companion, my travels became even more rich.

North had shown his usual skill in designing this being made of sticks. Since Twiner was made from the cuttings of Warrior's Willow, he had the valiant heart and protective soul of that most remarkable of trees. Through him, I learned the language of trees and leaves, of wind and rain and all the natural world. These elements became my comrades and vowed to help me fight whatever assassins Pitch might send against me.

But I was so enthralled with these days of *just being* that any worries about Pitch barely found a place in my thoughts. I knew now that I would have ample warning when danger was near—my left hand would be my alarm. Twiner called it "a wound that bonds" because although this wound gave me notice of trouble, it was also how Pitch could track and find me. So, yes, this wound would bond me to Pitch, for good *and* for ill.

As we walked through a majestic stand of chestnut trees, Twiner took my right hand firmly in his. "I was made to be an advantage," he said as slender branches sprang from the fingers of his right hand and twined firmly around my right fist and forearm. I was surprised—and a little alarmed.

"Your left hand is bound to darkness by your own bravery and compassion," he explained. "Now your right hand will be bound to light, by friendship and duty." Then he shoved the tip of his forefinger into my right palm and, with a quick jerk, broke it off. Yes, it hurt to have a three-quarter-inch piece of stick in my hand, but before I could protest or shout, Twiner smoothed my palm with a cluster of small, vivid green leaves that now sprouted from the tip of his broken finger.

"This will stop the pain and heal the scar," he said.

The chestnut trees around us began to sway. The rustling of a hundred thousand leaves created a rolling gale of sound that continued to echo from farther and farther away.

Then the branches from Twiner's fingers loosened and receded. Twiner let go of my hand and bowed.

"You are now connected to every tree that grows!" He kneeled at my feet. "You are their sovereign lord and friend."

The air around us—indeed, the sky all the way to the clouds—became filled with drifting leaves, millions and millions of them falling like snow for as far as any eye could see.

I had not seen this in my Moondream, but it felt like a dream. A glorious dream.

In the days that followed, we found ourselves in an increasingly wild landscape. The forests were ancient, dense, and enchantingly eerie. The ground was uneven and rocky, which slowed our pace considerably. We made our way through valleys so deep that at noon they were dark as night, and up hills so steep, we often used tree roots like ladders.

I found the land fascinating, and part of my fascination came from the unshakable feeling that Twiner and I were being followed. The trees here would tell us nothing despite our asking, answering instead with the equivalent of muted laughter. (When a tree's leaves wave slightly or when you hear consistent creaking and groaning of limbs and there is no wind, chances are you are being laughed at by a tree. They may find your clothes ridiculous. Your hiking skills clumsy. Or your yodeling off-key. It is not cruel or teasing laughter. They are simply amused.)

But in this case, in *these* forests, we weren't entirely sure. Even Twiner was stumped. These trees evidently had an alliance with some being that set them outside of the general brotherhood of large fauna.

The same held for the forest creatures.

None would talk to me. I tried to engage in conversation with an elk, a moose, three bears, and finally a gathering of chipmunks that were obviously very amused by us. The only word I managed to pry from the most giggly chipmunk sounded like "shadowbent." The word meant nothing to me.

But Twiner knew exactly what it meant. The moment he heard the word, he transformed into a bow and a quiver of arrows and instructed me to hold him at the ready.

The chipmunk broke into laughter.

"Twiner?" I asked, thoroughly confused.

"Yep?"

"I assume you will eventually tell me what 'shadowbent' is?"

"No need, really," he said in his usual, dry-as-a-stick way. "He stands before you."

I looked ahead and saw nothing, only massive chestnut trees, ground, and shadows. But then something caught my eye. A shadow that was distinct and appeared to move slowly and gracefully toward us. At first I thought it was a gigantic wolf, but as it came closer, the shadow stood upright and doubled in height.

"Aim at the shadow, please," muttered Twiner as if he were talking to a not-very-smart child.

I did as he asked, though I didn't feel that we were in any danger. There were no signs. My hand didn't hurt. There was no wind. And those silly chipmunks were still laughing.

As I drew my bow, the shadow came ever closer. It stopped, and at last it seemed to come into focus. It was, apparently, a man. He lowered his black hood to reveal a most distinguished face and head with a wild rage of extraordinary furlike hair.

"No need for weapons," said the shadow man in a thick Carpathian accent. "I am Shadowbent, and I mean you no harm."

From behind the tree trunks, a solid bank of hulking wolves now crept forward—more wolves than I could count or comprehend. They lifted their heads in unison and let out a collective howl that set my hair tingling. Then all the trees began to wave, and the chipmunks squealed; it seemed as

Skreevlick Shadowbent, king of the werewolves

if every living thing in these wild woods was signaling to us that Shadowbent was indeed the ruler of these lands.

Shadowbent was a gracious host. He took us to the crumbling, ancient castle that served as his home and made sure I was fed. Twiner took the form of a staff and listened to our conversation intently, never letting me set him out of reach.

Despite its disrepair, Castle Shadowbent was a regal and fascinating place. Set on the edge of the highest peak in the Carpathian Mountains, the views from its rooms and battlements inspired awe. A full moon illuminated the fog-shrouded valleys below and gave an enchanting shimmer to the untamed landscape of mountains and forests.

After dining, Shadowbent took me to his observatory, where a large, ornate telescope stood among the fallen stones and timbers of the castle's main tower. There were wolves in every room and hallway, pacing quietly, never taking their eyes from me.

"My men and I are forever bound to the Moon," said Shadowbent, gesturing to the wolves.

"Werewolves?" I asked.

Shadowbent smiled. "Yes. But not the werewolves you've heard of in stories." He sat in a large, throne-like chair that served as the observation seat for the telescope eyepiece. A dozen or so wolves padded over and reclined on the floor around him.

"We are men who became beasts to defend the weak. There are ancient evils in these mountains. Powerful families who have made misery for generations. We are savage men who savage others. The Moon gives us our power to summon justice."

Then he motioned toward the telescope.

"We have seen your battles on the Moon. Your battle with the one called Pitch." He leaned forward. "Pitch is not like us. He is a man who has become a beast and prefers to be a beast. He *wants* to stay a beast."

Suddenly, every wolf in the room stirred. They all looked toward the same opening in the tower wall, snarling. My wounded hand clenched in pain.

Twiner was in my other hand faster than a thought as a barrage of black arrows came streaming at me. But Shadowbent was faster still. With a snap, he whirled his heavy fur cape up like a protective shield. Every arrow lodged in his cape and came no closer.

Again I am saved by a cape, I thought, remembering Ombric's cape during Bright Night.

The arrows were only the first wave of the attack.

Through each crack in the tower walls poured sword-wielding black creatures.

"Nightmare Men!" I shouted.

The wolves sprang at them. Their werewolf fangs tore at the dark specters like razors against rag dolls. No sword made a single wound against the wolves, and the battle was finished before Shadowbent's cape could fall limp under the weight of the black arrows.

Except for the muffled growls of the wolves as they pawed and sniffed at the vanishing rags of the slaughtered Nightmare Men, the room grew quiet. Shadowbent turned to me.

"Pitch will never stop. Imprisoned he may be, but he will send whatever he can against you. He will do you hurt in any way he can so that you cannot hurt *him* again."

Shadowbent yanked a black arrow from his cape and pointed it at the secret pocket where I kept Pitch's dagger of tears. He touched the tip of the arrow to the pocket. There was a flash of light, and the arrow vaporized.

"But these will be his undoing," he said knowingly. "These tears are the last bits of his soul. The only thing left of him that is human. They are the weapon he fears most."

The wolves began to howl, but surprisingly, Shadowbent smiled at me.

"An interesting night?" he said.

I couldn't help but smile back.

Shadowbent's castle suited me more than I expected. The tower where I stayed had only half of its peaked roof intact, but as with a skylight, it gave me the opportunity to gaze at the Moon. My room was carpeted in decades' worth of fallen leaves. Here and there, a fragment of a broken stone archway jutted up from the soft, brittle dunes of the leaves.

The evening air was cool but not cold, and an easy breeze stirred a constant, dry rustle of leaf against leaf. Twiner leaned lightly against my hand with his crook up and kept watch. We were listening to the leaves as they told us the history of these woods and of Shadowbent and his werewolves.

"They are tragic men," said Twiner. "They have all lost their families to war, starvation, enslavement. Now they live to fight injustice."

"Yes," I said. "And why did they fight to protect me?"

For a while, Twiner was silent. Then, finally, he said, "They understand the power of your dream."

I wondered about this. Werewolves and men and families and myself. Twiner knew I was in a jumble of thoughts.

"You dream of a family you've never known." He added, "They dream of the families they have lost. *Your fight,* they said, *is the same as ours.*"

I thought about that answer for some time. It kept me from sleeping. But as I looked up at my old friend in the Moon, I felt him, if not speaking to me, then somehow sending me a feeling. The feeling that the leaves were correct, that, yes, in the many past chapters of my life as Nightlight, I had fought for justice. But now I was not so sure. What I fought for was not revealed in my Moondream. But then neither was Shadowbent and his army of werewolves. This part of my journey was a mystery.

As I drifted into sleep at last, the leaves said over and over, *Your fight is our fight*, till it became like a song.

And my dreams were gentle and my sleep peaceful.

Shadowbent and his men would be our escort until I reached the farm I'd seen in my Moondream. I had described it to him, and he made a deep, almost-amusing sort of growling sound.

"I know this farm," he told me. "It is outside our land but not far. We have kept watch on this family. They are very brave. Very kind. You have chosen well."

"I didn't choose them, really," I admitted. "I just saw them in my Moondream."

Shadowbent made the same pleased growling

sound. It is strange to hear a werewolf king laugh. It is a laugh that you won't ever forget. It starts like a growl but much deeper and slower. Then the steady rattle of the growl speeds up suddenly and stops with a high yip, then it all begins again with a slow build.

I found it to be at the edge of frightening. In short it pleased me enormously.

"Again I say, you chose well to end your journey with this family," Shadowbent said once his mirth died down.

"I told you I didn't choose them—"

"Kindness can be like a compass you did not know you carried," he said to me. "You are new to being human. I've been human and beast. Trust me, young friend, you chose well."

We traveled swiftly through Werewolf Valley and

the Transylvanian forests. The werewolves moved on all four legs, as did Shadowbent, and their paws made almost no sound on the soft, newly fallen snow. I ran among them, marveling at their stealthy grace as they moved through the woods like a silent stream.

Occasionally, I would use Twiner to pull myself up onto a low-hanging tree limb, and from there, I would follow the wolves from above, running and swinging from tree to tree. It was thrilling. I had never felt so free as in the company of these wolfmen. My mind was at peace. I became a being of pure action and instinct. I forgot about my past and my future, I forgot about heartbreaks or duty. I forgot about Pitch. I thought only of grabbing the next branch ahead of me and keeping up with my friends below.

For hours we went on like this, but I had no sense of time or its passage. I had not noticed that the sun had set and night had come and, with it, a heavy snow. But then we came to the edge of the seemingly endless woods. The wolves slowed, then stopped. Shadowbent stood high on two legs and pointed toward a clearing up ahead. Through the snow, I could see the lights of a house. The windows glowed with warmth. The house looked like a tiny, welcome ship in a sea of downy white.

My heart brightened.

I recognized these fields and the house from my Moondream!

I climbed down through the tree limbs and landed next to Shadowbent, feeling genuinely sorry to part from him.

"You'll need a new name to go with your new life," he told me, and I realized he had never actually called me by *any* name. It was as if Nightlight had never existed.

He shook my hand. It was the first time anyone had ever done that to me. He shook it the way I'd seen grown men shake hands, but I was still just a boy. He smiled at me and made his amused growling sound again.

"Within every boy there is a man, and in every man, the memory of a boy," he said. "Time to make the memories that will be your compass."

He let loose of my hand and gave me a gentle shove toward the house. Well, gentle for a werewolf king. So I walked toward the house I had dreamed of and the family who lived there and the boy named Jack whose life I had envied.

The werewolves howled as I walked away. They were saying good-bye. I took the last steps of my old life across the snow-covered field until I came to the threshold of what I would become.

As I walked toward the house, the only sound I heard was the gentle tapping of the millions of feather-size snowflakes as they landed. The snow fell so thickly that my footprints were erased as quickly as I made them.

"My past is vanishing behind me," I said musingly to Twiner, though he did not reply.

As I drew closer to the house, I could just make out talking and laughter coming from inside. I had seen these people, this family, in my Moondream, yet I had no idea what they sounded like. But I was able to easily discern each member of the family:

the mother, the father, the sister, and the boy I'd seen in my dream.

"It's time for me to be just a boy," I told Twiner. "To be as human as possible. No becoming invisible. No tricks . . ."

"And no Twiner being more than a staff?" he asked.

I nodded solemnly. "Unless I say so."

He paused as though he were thinking. "I understand," he said at last.

I looked inside a nearly frost-covered window. Snow, caught on the edges of the windowpanes, left me only an oval to see through. It was like looking at this scene through a dream, but now I was actually here! The only distance between myself and this family was this window between us—this thin sheet of cold glass.

They were at their dinner table. The plates were nearly clear of food, so I knew they had finished eating. I watched them as they talked. They seemed so happy in one another's presence. Then the boy glanced toward the window. His gaze stopped. His eyes went wide. For a fraction of a moment I almost made myself disappear—in fact, I may have, I'm not sure. Perhaps that's why the expression on his face was of such surprise. But then I knew I was visible because he pointed toward me and cried, "Look . . . there's a boy!"

The rest of the family turned and saw me.

Some moments in life seem to draw out, become longer than they actually are. This moment, this looking at each other through a pane of glass, was one of those times.

I could already discern so many things about

this family. They weren't frightened that a stranger was outside their house. They looked worried, not for themselves, but for *me*. They stood up quickly and came to the door. It was the father who opened it, but it was the mother who spoke first.

"Poor boy, you must be freezing," she said.

"Come in!" said the father. "Quick, before we all freeze."

I must have hesitated, because they reached for me and pulled me inside.

"He is frozen," cried the daughter.

"He's so frozen, he can't speak," cried the boy.

And then they were fussing over me, brushing the snow from my clothes and hair. I let the boy take Twiner. And the daughter took my cloak.

"Quick, Mother, get him some soup!" said the

father. They sat me down, and a bowl of soup was thrust in front of me and a spoon put in my hand. They stood around me expectantly. I just blinked at them. I was still so amazed to be with them and in this house. My Moondream had shown me this moment, but now it was *happening*.

"Eat!" they all said, but all I could do was stare at them.

"He's so frozen, he can't even eat," said the boy.

The mother sat next to me and put her hand gently on my shoulder. She leaned toward me, never letting her kind eyes break from mine, then she spoke very softly, as if she were speaking to a wounded bird. "Eat," she coaxed.

And so I began to eat.

I must have been very hungry. The bowl was quickly emptied, and now they were staring at *me*.

"What's your name?" asked the mother in her warm, tender voice.

What was my name? I had no answer.

"We are the Ardelean family. I am Victor," the father said with his palm on his chest, then he gestured to each of the others. "And this is my wife, Irina; my daughter, Ana; and my son, Jacklovich."

When I still did not offer up a name, Jacklovich said, "He's so frozen, he doesn't remember his name."

He was right in one regard: My mind was frozen. So much had happened. So much had led me to this place and these people. Wars had been fought and won. Moons had been nearly destroyed. The Golden Age had died, and yet I now sat in a simple wooden cabin with this kind and generous family who only wanted me to be warm and fed and to know my name. And I could not think of what I should be called.

I remembered that North had once said to Bunnymund, "My long-eared friend, you think too much. Difficult answers require a great deal of thought or none at all."

And so I spoke.

"My name is Jack . . . Jack Frost."

I said it without thought. It just spilled out. But I realize, now, that it made perfect sense.

"Jack," said the boy, delighted. "Like Jacklovich. Like me!"

In short order I was given an old nightshirt that had belonged to Victor, and the family began the ritual of going to bed.

No questions were asked as to where I'd come from or how long I'd been wandering. Perhaps they assumed I was just a bad-luck boy who'd lost his family. In the general excitement of being their guest it was decided I would sleep on a cot in the children's room, which pleased me very much. As I settled into the cot and under the heavy blankets that the mother had brought, Jacklovich never stopped talking.

"We will have so much fun. You will stay with us and be my best friend and we will have great adventures and—"

His parents came in.

"Hush, Jacklovich," said his father. "Our guest is tired and so are you." He must have been right, because the boy said nothing more. Then both parents hugged him and kissed him, and made sure his covers were up under his chin.

The scene stirred the most precious of my

Nightlight memories. The hug and the kiss good night was exactly how the mother and father Lunanoff had said good night to the baby Man in the Moon so long ago.

Then, incredibly, they came to me! First the father hugged and kissed me on the forehead, then the mother did the same.

"We hope you stay for a long time," said the mother, then they both left.

In all my centuries of life, in all those times I had seen the hug and the kiss good night, I had only watched. No mother or father had ever done those things to me. I knew their power; I knew that this ritual was a great protector of children during their journey through the night. But I had never once experienced it myself.

And this night I had.

The mother and father had taken me into their home, and by this simple act, they had made me feel something I had always longed to feel. I was not a protector or a warrior or a Guardian.

For the first time, I was cared for, not by friends or colleagues or wizards or kings or ancient stars above. I was cared for by beings more powerful, in their way, than all those others. I was cared for, *cared for*, by a mother and a father.

There is no care stronger in all the universe.

As I fell asleep, my mind had only one thought: *I am Jack Frost and I belong.*

I needed no dreams that night. Mine had come true.

The days that followed were a happy regimen of chores, play, eating, stories, and sleeping. Each of these activities was bound by two constants: friendship and imagination. From the very first morning onward, Jacklovich, Ana, and I were inseparable. We approached every activity as an adventure to be amplified by our collective imaginations. Milking a cow in a freezing barn was made memorable by becoming an improvised epic

in which the barn was a castle, the cow a magic beast, and the milk a life-saving elixir. Going from the barn to the house would become a journey in which we were hazarded by an ever-changing series of monsters, villains, armies, and enemies. Sometimes we would be wounded, sometimes we would be captured, sometimes one or all of us needed rescuing or saving or being miraculously brought back from the edge of death. Sometimes one of us would die and the other two would mourn with great conviction. Sometimes our grief was so unendurable that we would all drop dead in the snow until we got bored, and then, by some quirk of our own narrative logic, we would spring back to life and begin an entirely new drama with different terrors and triumphs.

For centuries I'd lived a life of relentless adventure

and I'd dreamed of quiet and normalcy. Now I had the quietest, most normal life imaginable, and I spent my every waking moment *inventing* danger and adventure—it was glorious.

Jacklovich, Ana, and I lived our lives in our daydreams. A unique type of bond forms among people whose exploits, hazards, and escapades are all pretend. We did not know what we would do in real danger, but oh my, how brave and selfless and grand we were as our pretend selves!

I remembered something that Ombric often said: "To understand pretending is to conquer all barriers of time and space." And now I understood what that really meant. We would be friends forever—Jacklovich, Ana, and I had sworn it, out on an ice-covered lake on the far edge of the farm. It was the scariest place we knew of, so we went there often. No grown-up could hear us from the center of the lake. And the ice was thinnest there. We would peer through the milky frozen water into the shadowy murk of the lake below and imagine all of our favorite horrors. For Jacklovich, it was ghosts and skeletons and vampires. For Ana, it was a sea serpent. And for myself? I would never—could never—tell my friends the truth of what I feared most. So I would always pause and make them wait until they couldn't stand my silence any longer and I would scream in mock terror, "A toy teddy bear!" or "Seven smiling kittens!" and they would fall down with laughter.

But one day we stood there, and Jacklovich, for no other reason than it seemed absolutely the thing to do, said with great seriousness, "We must swear by the thing that scares us most that we will be best friends forever and ever."

"I swear," said Ana and I.

"And I swear," said Jacklovich.

"And if we ever break the promise?" asked Ana.

"Then the thing that scares us most will come and get us," said Jacklovich. "But that will never happen," he added.

Such a wonderful perfection were we in our pretending.

We had no idea that we were being listened to by forces dark, ruthless, and unsympathetic.

That night as we were tucked into bed by Mr. and Mrs. Ardelean, I felt as happy as I ever had. Father Ardelean pulled back the rough cloth curtains of the room's only window.

"It is a full moon tonight," he told us. "It shall be your nightlight this eve."

Mother Ardelean said her good-night poem for us. She recited this poem most every night. Her lilting voice made everything she said seem strong and truthful.

> *"As the wide world sleeps*
> *keep these little ones safe.*
> *Keep their fears far away*
> *and their dreams bright till day*
> *so no hurt or harm or sorrow*
> *may ever come their way."*

Jacklovich and Ana always said the words along with their mother, and that night I did as well.

"That's the first time Jack said the night words with us," Ana remarked sleepily.

"I know," said Mother as she kissed Jacklovich and then Ana.

"He is part of the family now," said Father, then Mother leaned down and kissed me, too.

I closed my eyes. My old friend the Moon was *my* nightlight now. And I was Jack Frost of the family Ardelean.

Winter had been long, but the constant snow had been our ally. We had built a sort of snow castle out on the lake, complete with walls and even a tower. New snow added to the height and mass of our fortress, and the wind had sculpted it into fantastic curves and points. I wondered if Emily Jane had not lent a hand with the wind. Still, the fort reminded me of North's city and my Guardian friends.

I missed you all, but I knew that my life, my childhood life, was where I was meant to be.

Jack paused his story and looked at Katherine through the tangle of his bangs.

Katherine could tell that it was important to Jack that she understand this. She nodded reassuringly, and Jack looked relieved, then continued his tale.

Sometimes a week would go by before I had the chance to speak to Twiner, though he was always with me. On these rare times when I was alone, we spoke only briefly.

"Twiner, you still alive?"

"Of course," he would say.

"Just checking," I'd say.

"Are you still alive, Jack?"

"Of course."

"Just checking," he'd mutter.

We never slipped in front of the others. I had not revealed any of my old powers, and Twiner, true to his word, had stayed silent. So as far as my family knew, I was just a regular boy.

But the days had started growing longer and the snow fell less frequently. The ice would start melting. We knew that spring was coming and that our days at the fort would soon end. So we spent as much time there as we could.

Our last day seemed so ordinary. Which should have been a clue.

Farm chores are light in winter and we finished early, so we were able to trek to the fort after lunchtime. The weather had darkened, and the hope that we might have more snow cheered us. Perhaps the fort might last longer than we thought.

As we arrived, the wind began to pick up. Ana ran ahead. She always liked to raise our flag. There was a rickety tree limb that served as our pole, with my old blue shirt hanging from it.

I had come to love that flag. It was ragged and crude, but we had put our hearts into it, stitching

patterns of white thread around its sleeves and neck. We'd intended the patterns to look like snowflakes but we weren't very good at needlepoint, so it looked, well, not like snow. But it didn't matter. It was our flag, and *we* knew what it was supposed to be like.

Jacklovich and I were still twenty or so yards away from the castle as Ana raised the flag. It flapped in the now-steady breeze. The fort looked its best, all white and smooth. Ana waved to us.

"Hurry!" she shouted. "It's time to set sail!"

Ahh. Today the fort was to be a ship. I wondered where our minds would bring us today.

That was the last happy thought I would have for a long time.

As I raised my arm to wave back, I felt the unmistakable pain in my left hand. No! No! Not *here!* But there was no denying it—the pain was so sudden and sharp, it brought me to my knees.

"Are you all right?" asked Jacklovich, running toward me.

There wasn't time to answer. The wind had become a gale. I understood immediately that Emily Jane was trying to warn me. Then we heard the howling of wolves. Jacklovich looked around in alarm.

"They're coming to help us," I told him as he reached down to help me up.

"Help us? Why?"

The wind blew loose snow from the lake ice. Then the ice around us began to creak and groan. Thin, hair-width cracks appeared, making strange twanging sounds, as if a mile-long harp string had snapped.

"Run," I cried. "To Ana!"

The blowing snow added a peculiar haze to the terror that began to unfold. The ice gave a great groan and suddenly began to splinter and shatter in a path heading directly toward us. But I knew that this force was coming only for me.

"Get to the fort, now!" I yelled to Jacklovich.

He ran toward the fort, gripping and pulling me with him. I tried to break free—to keep him safe, I had to get away from him, but the thing under the ice was coming too fast.

"Twiner, get us out of here," I whispered urgently. The staff immediately responded. As the ice underneath us crumbled away, Twiner lengthened into a pole and vaulted us to safety inside the snow fort.

But not before we caught a glimpse of a hideous

creature that breached the ice. Long, foul looking, it was a nightmare incarnate.

"The Lermontoff Serpent," I said aloud.

"I should have known it was amphibious," remarked Twiner.

Jacklovich and Ana were gaping at me, speechless, clutching each other.

"There's a lot to explain but no time to do so," I told them, trying to keep my voice steady, trying not to frighten them even more than they already were. "Do as I say, and we might have a chance."

They nodded, but the situation was complicating more quickly than I could fathom. A gust of wind whirled the coating of snow from the ice, and we could see through it easily now. What we saw was dire. Hundreds of man-size shadows darted menacingly underneath the ice, surrounding not only the fort, but any path to solid ground. Meanwhile, the serpent had circled around and was swimming toward us once more.

"Are *these* the things you most fear, Jack?" asked Ana carefully.

"Yes, Ana," I admitted.

But I realized I had never feared what these creatures might do to Jacklovich and Ana.

Then Ana cried, "Look over there!" From the forested edge of the lake, werewolves were racing toward us across the ice, howling wildly.

"They are friends. I promise," I assured them. "You must go with them. Both of you."

"But what about you?" Jacklovich asked, his voice quavering.

The shadowy figures were circling in a frenzy under the ice at our feet. They made a horrible scraping sound—they were tearing away at the ice! They would break it apart within seconds. I had to lead the coming battle away from the fort if I wanted to save Jacklovich and Ana.

I pushed my friends up our small snow tower and waved at the werewolf leading the pack. It was Shadowbent, of that I was certain. I waved again, then pointed to my adopted brother and sister. I knew he understood.

There wasn't time to even hug them farewell. With Twiner in hand, I leaped from the tower and toward the path of the serpent. For these past months I'd not tested my old powers. I had buried them in the furthest reaches of my mind, in a place past memory, so I had no idea at this point how much they'd dimmed, how much they were intact. But now they flooded back. And with a fury.

I slammed the tip of Twiner upon the ice to announce my return, to let my enemies know their day would not go easy. The ice around me pulverized into a million arrowlike shards that made a target of the serpent.

The creature breached the ice, then dove deep to where my arrows had no chance to do any harm. But it gave me the opportunity to have Twiner aimed and ready. To my shock, however, the serpent did not come at me again. It swerved away and instead sped toward the snow fort. Then I realized with growing dread that the Nightmare Men had not followed me either, but were now breaking through the ice around and underneath the fort. In a blaze of speed Shadowbent and his werewolves galloped up to form a thick circle around Jacklovich and Ana, but they would be no match against the speeding serpent, which could sink the fort entirely.

I focused all my power to direct Emily Jane's winds; I had to get to them NOW. She did not fail me.

"Why does it attack the children and not me?" I asked Twiner as we flew above the lake, fast as light.

"What I think," said Twiner as he morphed into a long harpoon, "is too dark to say."

As we landed on the snow fort tower, I turned to Jacklovich and Ana, who looked so very scared. There were only seconds to spare.

"I am your brother and your friend. Always." I hugged them quickly.

Then I nodded to Shadowbent. He scooped the children up onto his back, then the whole pack of werewolves sprang from the fort and ran for the lake's edge just as one corner of the fort fell through the broken ice. The Nightmare Men's eyes glowed red with fury. One screeched, "Pitch will let you live, but he will kill all those for whom you care!"

My blood went cold. This was the truth Twiner could not say. Now that I was linked to Pitch, he would know, feel, be able to track down anyone with whom I formed a lasting bond, and send his Nightmare Men to kill them.

As the Nightmares moved to chase down Shadowbent and the children, the serpent crashed through the splintered ice beneath the fort and soared over me. Its jaws were opened wide and bore down on me. One quick glance assured me that the werewolves and the children had safely reached the lake's edge and were disappearing into the forest. So again I smashed Twiner down upon the ice, this time with a force that shattered everything that was frozen. The ice arrows were tenfold more than were needed to decimate every Nightmare Man and the serpent, but for me, they were not enough. I wanted Pitch to feel this loss. I willed the arrows to slice his men to ribbons, I covered every inch of his serpent with wounds deep enough to hurt but not kill. As the creature sank into the cold waters where my snow fort caved, I let myself be clamped in its jaws. Then I took the diamond dagger hidden in my coat and ended the serpent. I let myself sink with it to the dark, lonely bottom of the lake.

Because I knew what must be done.

There I would stay. Away from everything and everyone.

Pitch must believe I was dead so he could harm no one I loved.

I had to feel nothing. Be nothing.

I would become invisible.

Vanished. Gone.

I had taken one thing from the fort as it sank. My blue shirt, our flag. I held it tight in my hand.

For a hundred years I stayed there. For nearly all that time I thought no thought, I forced myself to never remember a moment or feel a single emotion. I would leave not a crumb for Pitch to follow. I could sense your sorrow, Katherine, at my being gone, but I could not let it into my heart. For Pitch would know and come for you. And in time I erased my memory. I forgot my whole life. I didn't remember Pitch. I was a book of empty pages. That's when I came back into the world. I knew I was different. I knew I had powers. Twiner kept my past a secret but stitched on the blue shirt

were three names: JACKLOVICH, ANA, and JACK
FROST.

I took the name that seemed right and began my
new journey. It was years before I remembered any
of *you*. That occurred on that last night in London,
with a different snow fight, when the Nightmare
Men tracked me down. Then I remembered everything. I knew someday I would need to use the
diamond dagger to face Pitch.

CHAPTER SIXTEEN

The Worm Turns Inside Out

It was close to dawn when Jack finished telling Katherine his story. The fire had gone from embers to ash, and the room was nearly dark.

She looked down at his left hand, wincing at the sight of the black scar there. It was so deep. She reached out her hand and placed it on his palm. Slowly, his fingers wrapped around and enfolded hers. They sat there together for some time. The things that could have been said would remain unspoken. She understood so much now. To save his family, to save her, to save everyone he loved, Jack had had to vanish. To appear dead. But he had come back. Years had passed and Pitch had kept distant. But now she felt that this too had changed. And that Jack was ready.

"You know how to end this, don't you?" she asked him.

Jack looked at her and nodded.

"His tears," he said as he pulled the extraordinary diamond dagger from his belt and held it up to her. Katherine had seen the first diamond dagger, the one that he had made as Nightlight. That had been made from the tears of MiM as a baby and the children of Santoff Claussen. It even contained her own tears. Jack's ability to take the sorrows of others and forge them into a weapon of protection had always amazed her. But this weapon was different. It came from a different kind of sorrow. Not from the heartbreak of the innocent. This dagger was born out of a far more dismal pain. It came from loss and rage and hate. It reflected light within its diamond prisms, but also a darkness, bleak, black, and terrible to behold.

"For all these years I had to keep my distance," Jack said to her. "I could never be close to anyone for long. Pitch's war against my heart was a danger for you all. My care became a death sentence."

Then he asked a surprising question: "Do you remember the jewels from my Nightlight uniform?"

Katherine nodded emphatically. "Yes. I saved the last ones!"

Before Jack could explain himself further, a great

ruckus erupted from outside the library doors. Shouts and crashes and then the sounding of the general alarm. They turned toward the doors. Outwardly, Jack remained calm, but the room grew cold as ice.

"Do you have them with you?" he asked Katherine as easily as if he were asking if she had a handkerchief. She pulled a necklace out from under her blouse. Tied to it was the small velvet pouch that MiM had given her.

"I carry them always," she told him.

He held out one hand, never looking away from the door. "May I?"

The noise outside grew more violent. Katherine poured the jewels into Jack's waiting palm. With his thumb, he began to slide and snap them one by one into the handle of the dagger. They fit perfectly.

"Good. I remembered the sizes correctly," he said

with relief. "The dagger is finished. Let's see what all this commotion is about." He pointed Twiner at the doors, and they flew open instantly. To their shock, Katherine's Raconturk guards were fighting a swarming horde of warrior monkeys. Katherine hadn't seen these monkeys since the battle of Punjam Hy Loo, when Toothiana had become a Guardian.

"Use your battle words!" she commanded her guards. The Raconturks looked gleeful and immediately obliged, shouting in quick succession.

"*Thud!*"

"*Crack!*"

"*Smack!*"

"*Splat!*"

Every monkey in the entranceway was felled by the invisible onomatopoeic force of the words. Jack shook his head with a grin.

"That is such a good trick," he told Katherine as they raced to the next battle-filled room. "I wish I could do it."

"Try reading more," she replied archly.

"I've been too busy making that dagger," he retorted as they faced another swarm of monkeys. Jack froze them with a quick wave of Twiner, and they shattered onto the floor. He and Katherine made their way to the main balcony that overlooked all of the Isle of Ganderly. From there, they could see that the entire island was under attack.

"I've never liked those monkeys," Katherine said.

"North hated fighting them too," said Jack. "He said with humans you can anticipate what they'll do, but monkeys are insane."

"Why, thank you," said a suave voice from above.

They swung around. They recognized the voice,

but not the creature from which it came. Lampwick Iddock of the Many Legs stood just over them on one of the many giant tree limbs entwined around Ganderly. With him was Blandim the Worm Boy. Clusters of monkeys squatted on every branch and patch of roof, poised to pounce.

"Monkey logic *does* have its advantages," said Iddock, his tail emerging from behind his elegant overcoat. It curled and twined as he peered down at them.

"The Monkey King returns," Jack said with a laugh. "I remember your voice. We fought you and your monkey army in Punjam Hy Loo! You've changed, Your Majesty."

"Yes," said Iddock, twirling the mustache that grew from his humanish face. "There have been improvements." Then he looked at his many legs. "And complications."

Blandim giggled in his boyishly wormy way, to which Iddock shot him a look of annoyance.

Iddock continued. "Pitch is a ... 'fanciful' employer."

"One way to put it," Jack agreed. "At least you are trending back toward human. Worm boy there, he's got a long way back to whatever he might have been."

"I like being a worm," said Blandim with a slightly confused frown. "Blandim good worm."

Before Jack and Katherine could fully stifle their snickering, Blandim brandished a small, pencil-like stick and started tracing shapes in the air. A thread of silk followed the tracings, and the outlines of butterflies and unicorns began to appear, suspended in the air. The effect was charming. Blandim smiled at Jack and Katherine and, astonished, they both smiled back. Then Blandim leaned forward, puffed up his cheeks, and blew. The silk drawings drifted gently toward them. Katherine reached out to touch a unicorn.

Twiner shook in Jack's hand. Jack understood immediately—Twiner sensed something sinister hiding within the silken whimsy. Jack blocked Katherine's fingers with the staff to keep her from touching the shape.

There was an immediate burst and sizzle of smoke—the silken drawings were like threads of acid. Blandim smiled his bland smile and giggled his bland giggle.

"I apologize," said Iddock, "but we do have our orders."

"You're too late," Jack said lightly.

He yanked the diamond dagger from his belt and held it, handle out, toward Iddock. Now it was Iddock's and Blandim's turn to look surprised. Both hesitated.

"I know Pitch has been able to read my thoughts since I got this scar." Jack showed them the ancient wound. "I also know he hoped to stop this dagger from ever being finished. And I know why."

He flipped the dagger and grabbed its newly jeweled handle with his good hand, then held out his scarred hand out so they could see it clearly. Katherine glanced at Jack uneasily. His only movement was to grip the dagger even more tightly.

Then, with a single quick slice, he cut across his scar. He pressed the blade of the dagger on the cut. A thin stream of black blood trickled from the reopened wound.

Even the monkeys flinched. The battle below stopped. Lampwick Iddock, Blandim, and every ape in their army clutched at their hearts. Jack's theory—the one he'd learned to keep locked in the most secret part of his mind and memory—was correct. All of Pitch's creatures were connected to his black heart. This dagger, made of Pitch's tears, could hurt his heart as no weapon ever forged—and if Pitch felt this pain, then so must all of his minions.

"As much as that hurts you, it hurts Pitch a thousand times more," Jack said in a steady, firm voice. The ground beneath them began to shake. It was as if the entire Earth were shuddering. "That's your master," said Jack to Iddock and Blandim. "He's very angry."

Jack then pulled the dagger blade away from his hand. The rumbling ceased. Iddock and Blandim no longer clutched their chests. The monkey army relaxed just a little. Again Jack flipped the dagger and held the handle out to Iddock.

"Take it," he said politely. "Your master will be most pleased. It's the only thing that can kill him. He certainly doesn't want *me* to have it. I could have him squirming in agony anytime I want. Forever."

Jack continued to hold the dagger toward Iddock. "Try to be more of a man and less of a monkey, for once."

Iddock grew red with outrage at the insult, but he was also tempted. He reached out, then hesitated.

"Blandim, my dear friend," he said to the worm boy. "You should have the honor. Go ahead." Blandim was delighted. He wiggled every finger in anticipation. He lowered himself with a wormy strand of his thickening silk and reached for the dagger. After a moment of happy giggling he grabbed the handle.

The explosion that followed was instantaneous. The dagger somersaulted into the air, and as it fell back down, Jack caught it as casually as a flipped coin. When the smoke cleared, all that was left of the worm was a pile of scorched clothes, and barely visible on the brim of his still-smoldering hat was a very small, squirming, little cream-colored . . . thing.

"He's . . . a grub," gasped Katherine.

"He's a maggot," Iddock clarified.

"Indeed he is," Jack confirmed.

Iddock gave Jack an appraising look. "I assume that you're the only one who can hold the dagger?"

"In this or any world," said Jack. "I'm the only one who can hold it or use it. And that is exactly what I intend to do."

He leaped up to a branch and grabbed Iddock by the lapel of his coat. With his face an inch away from the monkey man's, he spoke quickly and in almost a whisper. "I've fought your master for more centuries than you'll ever be able to count. I watched him destroy galaxies, worlds, civilizations, families, and friends. He's chased me and those I love across oceans of time. But I. Am. Done. I'm going back to the place where I was told I would never be rid of him. He'll know where I'm talking about. He can bring all his armies, everything that crawls or walks or flies. I'll be there waiting." Jack brought the tip of the dagger millimeters from Iddock's nose. The monkey man pulled away as best he could. Jack let loose of his lapel, and Iddock nearly tumbled from the tree limb.

Jack jumped down to the balcony with his usual matchless grace.

"Katherine?" he said, rejoining her and the troop of Raconturks who had gathered around.

"Yes, Jack?"

"Can your men send these fellows on their way?"

"How far?"

"Other side of the world?"

Katherine nodded. Like Jack, she knew exactly what to do.

She gave her men a single, sharp command: "Battle words, full power!"

In perfect unison the Raconturks shouted two distinctive syllables in their loudest voices.

"KAAAAAAAAAA-BOOOOOOOOOOM!!!"

Lampwick Iddock, the tiny maggot that was now Blandim, and their entire monkey army were blasted into the evening sky and out of sight. Jack tucked the diamond dagger back in his belt as he looked into the empty air where their enemies had vanished.

"Such a good trick," he murmured.

CHAPTER SEVENTEEN

Jack Is Nimble; Pitch Now Trembles

PITCH HAD LISTENED TO everything that had been said or thought by Katherine and Jack. For years he had focused his mind on the blood bond with Jack. The boy, that blasted boy, had shown compassion by stopping North's sword at the end of Bright Night. And ever since, Pitch had used this bond, cultivated it to the point where he could feel and sense Jack's every emotion. But Jack had been very clever. Yes. Pitch had truly believed that the boy had died in the icy waters of the lake. It wasn't until Jack began his gallivanting in London that Pitch felt his return. And since then, Jack had been so very careful to keep his plans secret. But now he had purposely let Pitch know everything—that he had completed construction of the dagger and he had understood the full power of such a weapon. And made very sure that Pitch knew he intended to use it.

Pitch's fury was felt throughout Santoff Claussen. Even Mother Nature was alarmed by the abrupt quaking that emanated from underneath the village. Every creature, human or otherwise, had gathered and were ready to do battle if Pitch attempted to escape. Then the shaking and rumbling stopped as quickly as it had started. The sudden silence was even more frightening. Emily Jane stood on the topmost branch of Big Root and listened intently to the wind and leaves. The Mythosphere was in use. She was astonished by what she heard.

"We are to stand down," she told the now equally astonished villagers. "We are . . . to let Pitch go."

"By whose order?" asked the Spirit of the Forest, so agitated she couldn't keep her feet on the ground.

"Jack Frost himself," Mother Nature replied. Her bewilderment was profound, but her faith in Jack was stronger, so she continued. "Furthermore, you and I are to rally the fairy nations to escort my father and his armies to a castle in Transylvania."

"This sounds terribly dangerous," said the Spirit of the Forest, her eyes glistening. She loved battles, especially when the fairy nations were asked to leave their forests and join in. "The nations of the wee folk will gladly do their part!" she assured Emily Jane. She waved toward the sky; it was already filling with countless leaves, each one guided by troops of Leaf People, the fiercest of all the fairy folk warriors.

A fairy folk warrior

Emily Jane hoped that the Spirit and the fairies would keep her father in check, and if she knew what Jack was planning, she did not let on. She was not acting as the daughter of Pitch, but as Mother Nature, who would do whatever was necessary to protect the world and its children.

CHAPTER EIGHTEEN

One for All
and All Against One

MEANWHILE, NORTH, BUNNYMUND, TOOTH, Sandy had gathered hurriedly at the top of the world to discuss the unsettling events. They had all heard the stories that Katherine and Jack had shared.

"What does that boy think he's doing?!" bellowed North. "Letting Pitch loose with his army? And sending us all to Transylvania, of all places!"

"It's a curious choice," Bunnymund admitted. He was twisting and untwisting his ears in concentration. "Surely, though, Jack must have some sort of plan."

Toothiana rubbed at her ruby pendant. "We have always underestimated him," she said thoughtfully. "And like it or not, we have misunderstood him. All those years he kept his distance . . . to keep us safe."

Sandy nodded, his Dreamsand swirling lazily around his head.

"What *do* you suppose Ombric told him back on Christmas Day?" asked North.

"We may never know for sure," Bunnymund ventured, "and I'm not sure if it would matter."

Yet they sat there wondering. So much was uncertain. Everything they'd spent centuries trying to accomplish now seemed to hang in the balance, and the scales were tipping wildly.

"In my experience knowing the particulars of a mystery is far less important than how things turn out in the end," Bunnymund added philosophically.

North turned and stared at the Pooka.

"Bunnymund."

"Yes, North?"

"You are the oldest creature in this room?"

"Oh, certainly," said the Pooka. "More likely the oldest creature in the known universe, I believe."

North reached over and unwound the rabbit's ears. "And that's the first entirely un-rabbity thing you've ever said."

"Thank you!" said Bunnymund.

North rewound his friend's ears with an irritated flick of his wrist. "The old hopper is right!" North boomed. "We know who our enemy is, we know where to fight him, so let's get going!"

They rose from their chairs and, feeling galvanized, almost jolly, began their journey to face old foes and help good friends.

"This is just what the proverbial doctor ordered," said Bunnymund.

Yet again the Pooka was right.

MEANWHILE, THE MAN IN the Moon stood alone looking around the beautiful room that had once been his nursery. Not a thing had ever been changed since those long-ago days, so it was like going back in time. MiM remembered everything from his past, which was a treasure both sweet and bitter. Joy and sorrow had equal purchase in his memory. But his memories of his days and nights in this room were almost entirely happy. The hugs and the kisses good night from his mother and father, followed by the ever-watchful Nightlight and his Dreamsand and his good-night song. Nightlight. His first friend. His oldest friend. His friend was much changed now, in name and in appearance, but one thing had stayed absolutely the same: Whether he was called Nightlight or Jack Frost, he was still the bravest boy there had ever been.

MiM had no room for worry. He knew that the Moon would be full and bright on the night when his friend would need him most.

CHAPTER TWENTY

Between the Tick and the Tock

MEANWHILE, OMBRIC WAS STILL recovering his strength as the drama he had set in motion played out. As Father Time, he was now everywhere and nowhere. He rested in the space between the tick and the tock. A place where events had started but had not yet finished. It was a peaceful place. Nothing moved or made a sound. A bird's song was not yet heard. A raindrop was waiting to fall. Lightning was soon to strike. But Ombric was certain that when the right moment came, Jack Frost would do his best. And that is all that a great wizard could ever hope for.

CHAPTER TWENTY-ONE

Like an Elephant Stamps a Flea

THE RAGE OF AN adult who has been outsmarted by someone younger is distinct from the many angers of the so-called grown-up. This rage is bitter. It is generously spiced with indignation and insult. Pitch felt all these variations of outrage. He felt them in the extreme. He felt them to the depths of his dark and dangerous soul.

But he kept silent.

As his ebony tomb peeled away and slowly rematerialized into his Nightmare Army, he stood erect but said not a word. His daughter greeted him coldly.

"Follow me. Tell your army to do as I say or you'll face the consequences."

With the meagerest of nods, Pitch agreed. His army fell into line behind him as he followed Emily Jane, who led them up through the dark, glistening tunnel of dark matter and toward the Earth's surface. Pitch kept one hand on his chest over the wound North had given him—the wound that was meant to kill him. The pain of Jack Frost's demonstration with the dagger still radiated around his heart. Pitch seethed with silent hatred. He had been so patient. He had planned his escape and revenge so thoroughly. And to what end? Complete humiliation at the hands of this eternal boy.

He was so clever, Pitch fumed. *He wiped his memory clean of anything that might help me. He only let me hear his misdirection. His real plans he kept hidden even to himself.*

As Emily Jane now ushered them out of the tunnel,
Pitch saw the full extent of Jack's and the Guardians'
growing power. Millions of leaves manned by the tree

fairies churned above Santoff Claussen. The leaves spiraled into a seemingly endless tunnel up into the sky. Though it was near midnight, the cloudless evening glowed with waves of aurora-like light.

Mother Goose's Mythosphere, I suppose. Pitch narrowed his eyes. Though this display was meant to prevent Pitch from escaping, it had the further effect of humbling him.

Then he saw the citizens of Santoff Claussen. He'd terrorized them for generations, but he saw not a lick of fear on any face he looked upon. Not on any man, woman, child, squirrel, or insect. And for the first time in centuries, Pitch felt, for one instant, a flicker of fear himself.

He stamped this feeling out like an elephant stamps a flea.

With the wind at her command, Emily Jane sent

her father and his army blowing through the tunnel of leaf fairies toward Transylvania. She followed close behind, full of hope for the first time in a very, very long time. She trusted Jack to not only protect the children of Earth, but to somehow bring her father back to a life that cast no darkness on the world.

But her father had one last trick—something Jack had revealed in his long story to Katherine and one he was certain that Frost would not be ready for.

CHAPTER TWENTY-TWO

The Greatest Strength

JACK EXPLAINED HIS OBJECTIVES in very simple terms to the Guardians and to Shadowbent. He had gathered his friends in the high tower of the Werewolf King's castle.

Jack held up his dagger. "Pitch comes to destroy me, to render this dagger useless, and then destroy us all." North looked to Tooth, who looked to Sandy, who looked to Bunnymund, who looked to Katherine, who looked back to North. None but Katherine had seen its final form, and they were awed by its sinister brilliance.

"In all his years of confinement his hate has grown ever stronger. Even our combined relics cannot destroy him," Jack said. "But this dagger . . . this dagger will end him."

"And how?" asked North.

"It is made of his sorrow," Jack explained. "And his sadness is what fuels all his hate."

Jack placed the weapon flat upon Shadowbent's massive dining table. The blade began to quiver, then move by an unseen force, its tip rotating till it pointed due south.

"It will always point to Pitch. To his hate-filled heart," Jack explained. "Katherine, take out the compass North gave you and see where it points."

Katherine was startled, but she pulled the beautiful compass from a pocket in her skirt. She had carried it without fail ever since North had given it to her when she was a child. It pointed toward North himself, so she could always find him. North smiled at the sight of the old gift. But his smile quickly fell to a frown.

The compass needle turned from him and pointed south.

"His hate has become so power- ful, it can retard even the purest good," said Jack grimly. He paused and let that statement speak to each of them. They understood what he was saying without his having to explain.

"I cannot tell you my plan, only my goal," Jack now told them, his voice echoing out from the tower and down into the valley and forests below. He took a deep breath before continuing. "Pitch must be stopped." His voice had a certainty that caused the other Guardians to look at Jack anew. Jack sheathed his dagger.

He was at this moment the strongest of them all.

Today he was their leader.

Each Guardian army was in position. Bunnymund's Warrior Eggs surrounded the base of the castle. With their armor-plated eggshells, they would be a tough defense to crack. With them were the great holy men warriors of the Himalayas, the Lunar Lamas.

Such a strange mix of troops—serene priests in their V-shaped formations, hands tucked in the sleeves of their robes, their faces squinting with blissful grins. And standing side by side were the various Yeti tribes.

In the woods that surrounded the castle the Spirit of the Forest lay in wait with every animal and insect with whom she was kindred. Untold millions of ants, beetles, snails, and centipedes were grouped in hidden masses awaiting the order to swarm. Legions of battle-ready squirrels and chipmunks, ten thousand birds, and even the grand old owls of Ombric's library roosted in the trees of Werewolf Valley.

The Tooth Fairy armies were positioned inside the castle itself. They waited in orderly groups by every window, ready to fly out to battle Pitch's airborne Nightmare Men if they attacked.

Katherine's Raconturks stood outside every

tower and wall, braced to shout their battle words. Shadowbent kept his werewolves inside the castle, where they crowded the doorways and passages. They were the last and fiercest line of defense, and Jack was thankful they were there.

"Thank you, my friend," Jack said to the Werewolf King. "If you hadn't taken me in all those years ago, I'd still be wandering, or even dead."

Shadowbent snorted his peculiar werewolf laugh. "Nonsense. But you should visit more often. You always bring a party."

"I like this royal wolfman," North murmured to Bunnymund. "He's a bit furry, but he understands life."

Bunnymund twitched an ear in agreement, then asked Jack, "You met only once, more than a hundred years ago?"

They nodded.

"Friendship will always amaze me," the Pooka mused.

"You realize that you're almost becoming human yourself, Bunny," said North.

"Well, I know how to fix that," Bunnymund replied. He plucked one of his transformation chocolates out of his vest pocket and popped it into his mouth. Before three twitches of his impressive whiskers, E. Aster Bunnymund had grown a total of ten arms (five on each side) and carried not only nine large sabers, but also his relic, the elaborately carved egg mounted on the end of his ceremonial Pookan staff.

North looked at him with a hint of envy, for Bunnymund stood a good two feet taller than the rotund Cossack when he was in warrior rabbit mode.

"I need to invent a new kind of candy cane that will do the same for me," North groused. But he grew quickly serious because from the south came a distant droning sound. A breeze kicked up, fluttering battle flags. The Guardians looked to Jack.

"It's Emily Jane and the tree fairies," Jack announced.

"It's time," Katherine added.

They carefully, deliberately placed the four relics of the Golden Age together. North held out his sword, which had belonged to MiM's father, Tsar Lunar, the last ruler of the Golden Age, with its crescent-shaped orb at the tip. Bunnymund held out his egg-topped staff, which held the purest light in all the universe and could bring life from any darkness. Queen Toothiana brought forth her ruby box, fashioned from the ruby arrow that had nearly killed her parents and which held the Man in the Moon's baby teeth. Then Sandy came forward. He placed his hand in the center to sprinkle his Dreamsand, the fourth relic, with which he could destroy any nightmare and leave in its place a happy dream. Jack placed his hand on Katherine's, and together they cupped the relics, for Jack himself was the fifth and final relic, or he had been, when he was Nightlight. But now he was even more powerful. Then Twiner morphed into six sturdy strands that wrapped, vinelike, around each Guardian's hand. They all—North, Bunnymund, Sandy, Tooth, Jack, and Katherine—looked from one to the other.

Everything had changed since they'd first become Guardians and found these miraculous relics, and they could feel the change within themselves. They were older. They had, in different ways, grown up. But they had not lost their childhood selves.

And this was their greatest strength. As they felt their bond renew and become stronger, they could feel the radiant hate of Pitch spreading toward them. He had grown stronger too.

But Toothiana felt something more particular. She could feel her old enemy, the Monkey King. He was near, she could tell, and up to something wicked.

"Jack!" she said urgently.

"What is it, Tooth?"

"There's something we don't know. I'm sure of it," she replied. "Something that is meant to hurt you."

"Search it out," Jack told her. "But wait until I signal you." He thought for a moment. The pain in his hand was strangely different. It hurt in a way that harkened back to his earliest days as Jack Frost. Pitch was hiding something. His hate was blocking

Jack's view into his thoughts. Jack held Toothiana's hand tightly. She nodded and spread her wings.

"I'll go with you," Katherine cried out.

"No, Katherine," said Toothiana. "Your place is with Jack. Especially this day." Then she dove into the air and flew out the window to the sound of countless leaves and a desperate wind rippling the air.

The remaining Guardians rushed to watch. In the dim midnight light they could see that the tree fairies and Emily Jane were losing control of Pitch and his army as they descended on Shadowbent's castle. The Nightmare Men and Fearlings were spreading out and pushing against the fairy leaf armada.

CHAPTER TWENTY-THREE

Once Upon a Time . . .

JACK'S GAZE GREW STEELY as Pitch's troops billowed through the sky like a toxic cloud. The next few seconds were to become the most difficult of Jack's life. His mind and memories became as focused and sharp as the diamond dagger he now drew from its sheath.

Flashes of the past came to him.

The first time he had seen Pitch.

Centuries before, on the Moon. Pitch was reaching out to destroy the baby Prince Lunar.

Jack remembered the hate that illuminated Pitch's eyes then.

And now that hate flowed with a hundredfold more strength. It radiated from him like waves of deadly heat, scorching the nearest leaf fairies, forcing them farther and farther away. Even Emily Jane was being forced back. The Nightmare Men took the advantage and began to pull out their spears and bows.

Yes, Jack thought. *Pitch means not just to destroy me, but to destroy us all.*

He whispered to Twiner, "Do all that you can to protect those I care for."

"You can count on all my powers," his devoted friend replied. Then Jack almost fumbled his grip on Twiner—a blistering pain flared through his left hand.

Jack locked his eyes on the rip in the Nightmare King's coat. Underneath lay the wound that Jack had stanched with his own hand.

The pain was worse than any he'd felt before. It

took all of Jack's energy to raise his hand, raise it above his head. He walked to the edge of the ancient stone balcony. The balustrade was broken. No matter. Jack climbed atop its clutter and stood tall, chin set firm, statue-still. Then he held his palm outward so Pitch could see the scar.

Jack closed his eyes and summoned every ounce of mental strength he had to feel and know what Pitch was planning. At the same time, he was making the temperature drop. Ten, twenty, thirty degrees. Then forty. A frigid front of air began to crash against the heat of Pitch's hate, sparking a blizzard of snow that filled the air of Shadowbent's valley.

All around Jack, the battle was on the verge of beginning. The Guardians' many forces were poised, waiting for Jack's signal.

The werewolf army began to howl, as did the Yetis

and the countless woodland creatures. The owls of Big Root hooted and screeched as they lifted off their branches to dive toward Pitch's relentlessly expanding Nightmare Army. Adding to the building tempest of sound was North, shouting orders above the din. He called to his reindeer, the very ones he'd discovered all those years ago, and moments later they were rigged and ready, pulling and bucking on their reins, their breath making clouds of steam in the Frostian atmosphere.

Katherine looked to Jack. The combined armies of the Golden Age were girding for Armageddon all around him, yet he stood there on the balcony all alone.

He has been alone too much, she thought decisively. She could see the growing scorch of Pitch's hate. It tinted the sky an eerie red.

"We need all the help there is," she said, calming

Kailash, who, like the other creatures, was agitated. Katherine closed her eyes. She could sense the great pulsing energy of her Mythosphere. Perhaps the world's storytellers could tip the scales against Pitch's hate. She began her call for help with the mightiest words in story: "Once upon a time . . ." She repeated the phrase over and over, and with her mind, she sent the invitation for all the poets, fabulists, tall-talers, imagineers, and yarn-spinners to lend their agile imaginations to the cause. And they heard her. Whether sleeping or awake, her desperate call was heard, and the Mythosphere glowed brighter than it ever had. The boundaries of its strength were as yet untested. The way that the power of story could affect reality would soon be known.

CHAPTER TWENTY-FOUR

Mind Over What Matters

Jack's mind was so focused on what his foe was thinking that he was now unaware of anything else around him. There was such a churning clot of hate in Pitch's brain that it was difficult to discern any single thought, much less the one Jack sought. *There's something he doesn't want me to see,* was all he could surmise. *Something that could somehow be a trap.*

Jack was, however, purposely *letting* Pitch read his thoughts. It was the only way to keep the Nightmare King distracted from what Katherine and the others were up to.

Then he glimpsed a flash of something familiar lurking in Pitch's mind. Something from Jack's past. Something he loved very much. The old farm cabin, the one from his Moondream. *Where Ana and Jacklovich lived!* And the pain surging through his old wound grew so intense, he nearly plunged from the balcony.

The hardest part about being Jack Frost was outliving any mortal, no matter how loved they may have been. He had never dared to visit the Ardelean family again. The Nightmare King had sworn to kill all those Jack loved, so to keep them safe, he had stayed distant. But he knew they'd had good lives; the werewolves had watched over them and had reported on their history. Jacklovich had married and stayed on the farm. He'd raised many children, the eldest named Jack. And that boy had grown up and done likewise.

By now there had been three generations of Ardelean children named Jack. Ana, too, had married and lived nearby. She, too, had children. And every year the family celebrated Jack Frost's birthday. They used the day that he'd first said the "good-night words." Jack felt a flush of warmth at the memory.

The image transformed, and Jack began reeling once more. The Ardelean cabin was being surrounded by Lampwick Iddock's monkey army. Jack knew this was not a memory, but something that was actually happening.

As Jack thought frantically of what to do, Pitch's voice was suddenly in his mind.

"You thought I had forgotten about your beloved adopted family." The voice could almost be described as a tender whisper. It went on. "I was merely waiting for the right time to use them against you."

The image changed again. Now Jack could see inside the cabin. He could see a father, mother, and three children. Two girls and a boy of perhaps eleven who bore a striking resemblance to the original Jacklovich. All five were being held roughly by the largest of Lampwick's monkey soldiers.

The Monkey King and Blandim were there as well. Blandim was no longer a tiny maggot. He had grown into something closer in size to a baby squirrel.

He wore a little cloak and a childish sort of beanie. He was stumpy and slimy and still very much a worm, and now he was worming his way over to the children. With the same sinister twig that Jack had seen before, he began tracing through the air. Once again the silken shapes of flowers and unicorns appeared. Jack wanted to shout "Don't touch!" They were made of acid! But the children wouldn't be able to hear him. So with all his concentration, he sent out his call to Toothiana.

It was time to strike.

CHAPTER TWENTY-FIVE

No Mercy

Toothiana had a keen sense of good and evil. She was, after all, half Sister of Flight and half human. Of all the beings on Earth, the Sisters of Flight had the most developed sense of a creature's true nature. Being the sacred flying protectors of Punjam Hy Loo required that they had a heightened sense of danger, and for centuries the greatest danger they had felt was the nagging menace of the Monkey King.

So Toothiana needed only to breathe to locate Lampwick Iddock and his simian army.

She found them gathered at the Ardelean farm,

and she stealthily circled in the sky above till she heard Jack's mental call as distinctly as if he were hovering beside her. "Go!" was all he said, but that was all she needed.

She tucked her magnificent blue and green wings close and glanced up at the Moon. "Wish me luck, old friend," she whispered. Then she leaned into a dive, plummeting silently toward the cabin. Toothiana was not a vengeful being. She reserved the streak of animal ruthlessness in her nature for stopping the wicked. Her beautiful half-bird eyes glistened in the moonlight. There would be no mercy for the Monkey King tonight.

CHAPTER TWENTY-SIX

Sadness Into Snow

As everything hung in the balance, there were only seconds to act.

Hate and rage move at the speed of light, and before a single second had passed, Pitch had sent forth a searing red wave of fury that engulfed and blinded every creature that stood their ground in Werewolf Valley. The Nightmare Army that levitated around Pitch, bows tensed, now marked their targets.

By the next tick of the clock their deadly arrows would rain down on the blinded Guardian armies, who could not see the doom that was coming.

North, Bunnymund, Sandy, Katherine, and Jack—
none of them knew they were each targeted with an
arrow aimed at their hearts. In perfect unison every
Nightmare Man heard Pitch's command to let loose
their arrows. In the time between the tick and the
tock, all of the Guardians would die.

But . . .

Jack had already made his move.

Ombric Shalazar, the greatest wizard the world had
ever known, the figure who was now known as Father
Time, the man who knew the realm between the tick
and tock better than anyone, had seen this moment
coming. He could not violate the rule set down by the
Man in the Moon himself. He could not go forward
in time to help the Guardians or any living soul. The
future could not be tampered with or changed.

But . . .

The future could be planned for.

And that is what Ombric and Jack had done. At their last fateful Christmastime meeting, he had told Jack Frost only one thing. He had told Jack to "remember."

And Jack had. He had remembered so many things. He had remembered *everything*. He had remembered sadness and joy and everything in between. He remembered the kiss and the belief it gave him in Katherine. He remembered Pitch's tears. He remembered that those tears came from love and sorrow. And he remembered Emily Jane's belief in the goodness of her father. All those remembered things had guided him to this moment.

So as soon as Jack had sent word to Toothiana, he took the diamond dagger in his good hand. At the exact instant Pitch's wave of light blinded them, Jack, with a single thrust, speared his own scarred hand completely through, right at the center of the scar. He did it so quickly that he didn't feel any pain. But Pitch did. In less than a breath he crumpled. As did every soldier in his Nightmare Army. The blinding light of his hate extinguished. The sky shed its reddish hue, and the night returned to normal. But not before the black arrows of the Nightmare soldiers had been released. They streaked toward their targets. There was no time for any Guardian to respond.

In that blink of time miracles occurred.

Pitch, writhing in pain, began to fall from the snow-filled sky, and as he did, the arrows turned brittle, then emberlike. Their speed slowed.

Pitch landed hard on the cobblestone road outside Shadowbent's castle. His grounding barely made a sound.

The black arrows, once so deadly, were now so fragile that the falling snowflakes were enough to shatter them. With the glow of the Mythosphere, they dissolved to dust, making a faint chorus of sound, like a million whispered sighs.

The Nightmare Army still drifted above Werewolf Valley, but they too had become like cinders. The full Moon shined right through them. With a single gentle breeze from Katherine's Mythosphere, they broke apart, every last one of them, and dwindled till they were less than mist or even smoke. They evaporated in a silence that felt like peace.

Now they are just a story to be told, thought Katherine. *They are a part of the Mythosphere.*

She looked for Jack, but he was gone. She ran to the balcony. A spattering of black blood on the ruins of the stone rail vanished just as she spied it.

She could sense no feeling of Jack at all. Deeply afraid, she leaned over the balcony, searching for any sign of him.

She needn't have feared. He was down below, kneeling over the fallen form of Pitch. Across from him was Emily Jane, also on her knees. She was holding her father's hand, the one that had always clutched the painted cameo of her. North, Bunnymund, and Sandy had joined her. As had Shadowbent. The Guardian armies began to leave their battle lines, drawn toward the place where Pitch lay. They watched the final moments of the Nightmare King unfold.

With a sharp pull, Jack took the diamond dagger from his wounded hand. He gently placed that hand on Pitch's chest, just over his heart. Then he raised the dagger. For a moment it seemed he would stab Pitch, kill him, but he paused. As he held the dagger aloft, it seemed to melt—it *was* melting!—turning back into tears. Pitch's tears. They dripped slowly but steadily, landing on Jack's scarred hand.

The wound healed. No sign of it could be seen. The dagger dissolved completely. Even the jewels from Nightlight's uniform became liquid and seeped away.

Every teardrop that ran from Jack's hand began to soak into Pitch's chest. As the last drops vanished, so did Pitch. Or at least what Pitch had become. As the Guardians' greatest enemy lay in front of them, a great transformation occurred. The twisted grimace and sickly pallor of his face softened and smoothed, and for the first time since the Golden Age, the face of Kozmotis Pitchiner, Lord High General of the Galaxies, Tsar Lunanoff's first in command, was

The Lord Pitchiner

looked upon by the one person who loved him. Emily Jane leaned close to her father's face.

By now Katherine had come down from the castle and stood silently behind Jack. The Guardians together gazed at their fallen foe with a quiet reverence.

Sandy and Bunnymund were the first to kneel, their heads bowed. They had both known Pitch when he had been Lord Pitchiner.

Sandy had served under him before the dark days of the Nightmares and had worshipped the once-noble commander. Sandmen cannot cry, but Sandy looked as if he might.

"From what I know of humans and men," Bunnymund said solemnly, "he was, before his darkening, a man of greatness."

"Brave. Honorable. Selfless," whispered Emily Jane, blinking back tears.

"Then he deserves our respect," said North as he too dropped to one knee. As did the gathered armies; every Yeti, werewolf, fairy, Warrior Egg, squirrel, and bug. They kneeled in tribute to their ancient enemy. He was an enemy no more. Their war had saved him. The Nightmare King was gone. His hate and hurt were gone.

Jack's snow was still falling, but not a flake touched Lord Pitchiner.

"I did my best for him," Jack said quietly to Emily Jane.

She gave a slight smile. "You kept your promise."

Katherine looked from one to the other, a thought dawning. *They are both his children in a way,* she realized. *Neither would exist without him.*

She looked up at the cloudless sky and the falling snow. This snow, it was Jack's sorrow. *He was mourning his old enemy, and now he wishes him well,* she thought. *Like everything Jack faces, whether he knows it or not, he changes it. He turns darkness into light, wars into salvation, sadness into snow.*

CHAPTER TWENTY-SEVEN

Snag, Smush, and Whittle

TWINER HAD FLOWN TO the Ardelean farm as soon as Jack had given the Tooth Fairy the word to go. He had made himself into a bow and arrow and shot himself there. The bow part of him had grabbed the arrow part, and then the stick-man part of him grabbed the bow, and they morphed into a single well-shot arrow shaft that sped sixty miles with surprising accuracy. He shot himself straight through the keyhole of the Ardelean cabin door, instantly snagging the beanie off the head of Blandim the Worm Boy and destroying his evil unicorn tracings, which the youngest of the three generations of Jacks was unwittingly about to touch.

Thirty-three one hundredths of a second later Toothiana come crashing through the roof and landed on top of Blandim, successfully smushing him as one would smush a large slug.

The ensuing splatter was impressive and elicited a delighted "yuuuuck!" from the three Ardelean children. Jack III grinned as well.

Toothiana easily sidestepped the goo and spun around to face Lampwick Iddock.

"The flying half-breed makes her entrance," snorted Iddock in his most oily tone. "You fluttering harpy, I'll pluck your—" But before he could finish his insult, she had, with a single sweep of her sword, cut all eight of his legs off at the knees.

The limbs toppled over like bowling pins.

"That was rather harsh," Iddock blurted as he dropped several inches.

"What exactly are you supposed to be?" asked Toothiana with a hint of repulsion, taking in for the first time Iddock's evolution from maharaja to Monkey King to . . . what?

"Whenever I disappoint Pitch, he devolves me into something more embarrassing," Iddock muttered. "Last time he turned me into a monkey, but he added eight legs as sort of a joke."

Toothiana had to think about that one for a moment. Then she laughed. "Oh! Eight legs! A *spider* monkey!"

No sooner had she said this than Iddock turned to dust before her eyes, as did his monkey troops. Even the unsightly stain that had been Blandim dried up and disappeared.

Toothiana and Twiner looked at each other in astonishment. Twiner himself had shifted back to his scarecrow-like self. "I do believe this means Jack succeeded, and the Mythosphere has proved its worth."

Toothiana sheathed her swords and scuffed the floor where Iddock had stood.

"Indeed," she said absently. "Too bad he won so quickly. I enjoy whittling."

"Who *was* that eight-legged fellow?" asked Jack III.

"A wicked maharaja, a pathetic man, and a miserable monkey," she replied frankly.

"Oh," said Jack. His grin grew wider still.

CHAPTER TWENTY-EIGHT

Time and Tide

THE FULL MOON WAS low on the horizon. It would soon set behind the trees that surrounded Werewolf Valley to the west.

"I would like for you all to see my other family," Jack told the Guardians. North called for his sleigh. There was just enough room for everyone, even Shadowbent. It was the first time in centuries they had taken a ride together in that most elaborate and wondrous of contraptions.

Jack sat pensively in front, between North, who piloted his reindeer, and Katherine. It was an effort for her not to glance too often at Jack; she knew it would annoy him. Without intending to, they had both settled into the same age. Jack was the oldest he could ever appear—eighteen—and so was Katherine.

A light snow still fell. It was Jack's snow, certainly, but Katherine could feel that it came from a place inside his heart that she had never before known. It was a place of tranquility, perhaps even peace.

As the sleigh landed outside the Ardelean cabin, Shadowbent looked around appraisingly. "The snow. The cold. This is very like the night I brought you here for the first time," he said to Jack. And indeed it was.

Jack thought for a moment. "I went to the house alone," he said more to himself than to Shadowbent.

Toothiana and Twiner were standing outside the cabin to meet them. "All is tended to," Toothiana assured Jack as he leaped from the sleigh. The rest of the Guardians stayed put. This moment seemed to belong to Jack.

Boisterous sounds from inside the cabin caught their attention. The house was alive with light and warmth, just as it had been all those years ago. Jack's heart swelled as he walked hesitantly toward the front door. He paused to peek through the window. Once again he could barely see through the frost.

Then the door swung open, the warm inner glow lit the snowy night.

A boy stood silhouetted in the doorway. A wild-haired boy. Thin and willowy. Jack could just make out his face. The mischievous grin was there. It was a Jacklovich descendant, all right.

"You're him," said the boy with awe. "The boy they tell us to remember."

He grabbed Jack's hand. The one that had been

wounded all those years and wars ago but now was healed, the skin now smoothed of its wounds.

"And what do they tell you?" asked Jack as the boy began to tug him inside.

"That your name is Jack Frost."

"And?" Jack coaxed.

"And that you saved our family. And that you'd come back someday."

Then his sisters crowded the doorway. One grabbed Twiner, and the other pulled on Jack's other hand.

"They told us," said one sister, "that we should always believe in you."

"Even if we never see you," said the other.

Now Jack grinned. "And did you?"

"We believed! We believed! We believed!" the threesome shouted.

The Guardians, smiling from the shadows, recognized the echo of Ombric's first lesson in magic—to believe. They watched as Jack was drawn into the cabin, surrounded by children and parents, everyone talking excitedly at once. But Jack stopped just inside the door. Without looking back at the sleigh, he held out his healed hand.

"Come, Katherine," he said. "You must see how my story ends."

She smiled at her fellow Guardians, hopped from the sleigh, and joined Jack. As she took his hand, it dawned on her: *This is the beginning of his story, not the end.*

The snow was still falling, now in huge, feather-size flakes. The tracks of the sleigh and all their footprints would be lost and covered before the Moon set and the sun rose. But they would remember this moment for as long as they had breath. Perhaps longer.

"I think we'll know where to find Katherine and Jack when we need them," North remarked. Bunnymund nodded, as did Sandy, Toothiana, and Shadowbent. For an instant, they felt Ombric's presence. The great wizard could still work magic like no other.

With one last look, North called "Away!" to his reindeer. And each of them thought the same thought as they coursed through the sky and watched their mighty friend the Moon finally disappear at the world's edge.

No matter what may happen, through time and tide, through thick and thin, children will always believe.

The End

Acknowledgments

Publishing a novel is a long journey and a grand adventure. To me there is a nobility in the process and its traditions. The people who published this book are like a tribe of alchemists. I hereby thank, acknowledge, and celebrate:

Jeannie Ng, eagle-eyed copy editor;

Lauren Rille, lightning-fast designer extraordinaire;

Elizabeth Blake-Linn, production manager who gets everything all gorgeously printed with fancy specs;

Alex Borbolla, who goes over every little detail;

Anne Zafian, deputy publisher who Makes Stuff Happen;

Chrissy Noh, marketing visionary and jolly prankster;

Lauren Hoffman, head of marketing/publicity who has been championing the Guardians books from the get-go;

Lisa Moraleda, publicist who shouts from the rooftops;

Michelle Leo, head of library and education, and a saint;

and the Grand High Poobahs of the House,
Justin Chanda—wizard of whiskeys, roof farming, and books—
and Jon Anderson, the genial Guardian of the Creative Spirit

‹ W. J. ›

A Reading Group Guide to

THE GUARDIANS #5

JACK FROST

THE END BECOMES

THE BEGINNING

About the Book

Guardian Jack Frost is known throughout the world as a carefree, fun-loving character and a protector of children. But was his life always this way? Through interactions with Jack's many friends and enemies, readers learn the story of Nightlight, Jack's start as protector of the baby prince on the moon; Jack's epic battles with Pitch and his Nightmare Men; and Jack's transition into a new form known as Jack Overland Frost. Join Jack and his fellow Guardians as he keeps the children of the world safe from the atrocities inflicted by Pitch and his army, and tells tales of his beginnings.

Discussion Questions

1. When the story began, where was Jack? What was the date, and why was it so special? Explain why Jack was alarmed and what this caused him to do. How might you have reacted if you were in Jack's shoes?

2. Jack had several daggers in his home, but there were limitations on when and how these daggers could be used. What were these limitations,

and why do you think they existed? Discuss how these daggers were made and the importance of the dagger that was left unfinished.

3. As Jack prepared to leave his home to join his friends, he was attacked. Who warned him, who protected him, and how did he respond to this attack? How did this experience inform him that evil had returned?

4. What was the gift that North sent to Nightlight? What kind of impact did it have on the story? When encountering Lermontoff Serpent, what did Nightlight discover about himself and Twiner? Think about Twiner and his role in the book. What function did he serve, and how was he able to do his job?

5. Why did Katherine, aka Mother Goose, chronicle the histories of the Guardians? What had Katherine learned in her childhood about the power of stories? How does this compare to what you've learned about stories? Why are stories important to you? Do you have any stories that have been passed down through your family?

6. How important was it for Katherine to write about Nightlight and his fight with Pitch? Why was Pitch concerned about stories that did not describe histories, but were meant to be fun? Do you agree or disagree with his beliefs about stories? Name some stories that were said to be inspired by Jack Frost.

7. Emily Jane, Pitch's daughter, monitored Pitch's imprisonment. Her abilities had grown stronger

over the years, ensuring Pitch's inability to escape. How many years had Pitch been imprisoned before the start of this story? Why was Emily Jane willing to keep her father imprisoned, even though she loved him very much? Have you ever had to make a difficult decision involving someone you love? Explain why it was so difficult and how it made you feel.

8. The Great Depression caused chaos and fear throughout the world. What is a depression? How did it affect the Guardians, the Nightmare soldiers, and families everywhere? What problems did the Guardians have on Christmas Eve? Why didn't Jack help deliver the presents on Christmas Eve when it was one of his favorite activities? Do you think Jack regretted his choice?

9. Name all the Guardians and discuss their similarities and differences. How did they promote their individual earth holidays? Why did they think they'd be able to help the children grow up in ways that would allow them to become morally conscious adults? Discuss their concerns that children would stop believing and how that would impact their futures. What would you say to them to help allay their fears?

10. Discuss Ombric Shalazar and his radical transformation into Father Time. When and how did he change? On Christmas Eve, he was so agitated that only Jack could calm him. How did the two of them communicate, and why couldn't the other Guardians participate in the conversation?

11. The kiss between Katherine (the magic of humans) and Nightlight (the magic of the Golden Age) at the end of the War of Dreams formed an everlasting impression. Normally a kiss would bring two people closer together, yet with Katherine and Nightlight, something else happened. Discuss their relationship, and the fact that the Guardians noticed a change in Katherine after the kiss. What was the Guardians' conclusion? Do you agree with them? Would Katherine's kiss have had the same effect on another character?

12. Nightlight disappeared for one hundred years. Katherine started reading articles in a London paper describing an untamed, white-haired young person whose age changed from telling to telling

and whose name was Jackson Overland Frost. How did Katherine know Jackson Overland Frost was Nightlight? What happened to Katherine whenever she thought about Nightlight? Why had he come back?

13. What is an oath, and how sacred is it? What types of oaths have you taken, if any? Think about promises to your teacher, your classmates, your community. What happened once Nightlight fulfilled his oath? What happened to Katherine's Nightlight? What prevented him from having the normal life sequence of a Nightlight?

14. Nightlight stated: "To have no clue about one's fate is a strong and fearful feeling." Can you relate to this statement? Why do you think Nightlight felt this way? Explain your answers.

15. Why was it important for Nightlight to be out of communication with the other Guardians while he was evolving and continuing his Moondream?

16. Explain what Twiner meant when he called Nightlight's wound a "wound that bonds." How might a wound that bonds differ from a wound that doesn't bond? What did Twiner do to Nightlight to balance the bond? Explain what this action was supposed to do to Nightlight. Was it effective?

17. Jack encountered a man named Shadowbent on his journey to his dream family. Although Shadowbent looked menacing, Jack didn't feel threatened. Why do you think that was? What impact might Jack's previous experiences have had on this moment? Discuss Shadowbent's

story and his relationship to his fellow men. Shadowbent and Jack were unaware that they shared a common bond. What was it, and why do you think they failed to recognize it?

18. When Jack was adopted into the Ardelean family, he was immediately treated as part of the family. As he readied himself for bed, what ritual did his adoptive parents perform? Discuss this ritual and what it means to you. Would you have reacted similarly to or differently from Jack? What memories flooded back as Jack watched the ritual?

19. What was Jack learning during the activities he participated in with the Ardelean family? How important was imagination and play to the

development of Jack Frost? Explain your answer with examples from the book.

20. While Jack, Ana, and Jacklovich were playing on the icy pond by their snow ship, they were attacked by Lermontoff Serpent and hundreds of Nightmare Men. One of the Nightmare Men yelled to Jack, "Pitch will let you live, but he will kill all those for whom you care!" How did Jack respond to this attack? Once he knew his friends were safe, how did Jack convince Pitch that he was dead? What was the significance of the one item he took with him as he sank into the dark, lonely bottom of the lake? Describe Jack's character traits and skills that helped him to pull off this trick and save his friends.

21. After Katherine and Jack shared stories of the past one hundred years, there was a commotion outside the door. Jack showed Katherine the dagger made with Pitch's tears. What was different about this dagger compared to the daggers made from children's tears? Why did he show it to Katherine?

22. Jack asked Katherine if she still had the jewels from his Nightlight uniform, and she poured them into Jack's hand. What did Jack do with the jewels and his scar, and how did these acts affect the battle? What theory of Jack's did this prove? How did this knowledge help Jack?

23. How did Lampwick Iddock of the Many Legs trick Blandim the Worm Boy into taking Jack's dagger? What was the result of that action? What

did Iddock learn from this? What was so special about the dagger that, if used properly, ensured Pitch's end?

24. The rage Pitch felt at being outsmarted by a younger foe was distinctive compared to his many other angry moments. What was the difference? How was Pitch's fury felt throughout Santoff Claussen? Did you feel strongly that Pitch would be put in his place? Give examples from the book that clued you in to his fate.

25. Despite his situation, Pitch did not give up hope of winning the battle. What secret of Jack's did Pitch remember and plan to use against him? What caused Pitch to be afraid? What was his reaction to that feeling?

26. Emily Jane felt conflicted as she escorted her imprisoned father to Transylvania. What did Emily Jane hope would happen? Who do you think she would protect in a battle?

27. The Guardians decided they would follow Jack's instructions and meet in Transylvania for a battle with Pitch and his Nightmare Armies. Why do you think the Guardians, with all their wisdom and experience, were willing to follow Jack's lead? What does this tell you about Jack?

28. As Jack looked at each of his Guardian friends, he noticed that they had all aged, yet they had not lost their childhood selves. Discuss if this is possible—to be an adult and still a child at heart, and the effects it would have on your life.

29. Jack stated that Pitch's years of confinement made his hate stronger. Do you agree with him? Why do you think that is? Can you think of examples in the news or in your community where this is also the case? Is there anything we can do to stop this cycle?

30. Katherine could feel the energy in the Mythosphere. What was the Mythosphere? She wondered if the power of stories could tip the balance of the battle in their favor, and decided to try by repeating "Once upon a time." What effect did this have? Do you think stories have the power to change things? Consider both fictional and non-fictional stories in your answer.

31. On Christmas Eve, Ombric said one word: "remember." How important was the word "remember" to the outcome of the battle?

32. What action did Jack take to stop Pitch from starting the war? How did he know this action would work? What was Toothiana's assignment, and did she succeed in her mission?

33. Do you think Jack saved Pitch? What happened when Jack allowed Pitch's teardrops to soak into Pitch's chest? How did Pitch's secret plan to destroy Jack fail?

34. How important was friendship in this story? Did the Nightmare Men have any friendships? Did Pitch have any friends? How important are friends in real life? Explain what qualities you look for in a friend.